Cutting It Short

Bohumil Hrabal (1914–1997) was born and raised in Brno in what was then the Austro-Hungarian Empire. After working as a railway labourer, insurance agent, travelling salesman, manual labourer, paper-packer and stagehand, he published a collection of poetry that was quickly withdrawn by the communist regime. He went on to become one of the most important and most admired Czech writers of the twentieth century; his best-known books include *I Served the King of England*, *Closely Watched Trains* (made into an Academy Award-winning film directed by Jiri Menzel) and *Too Loud a Solitude*. He fell to his death from the fifth floor of a Prague hospital, apparently trying to feed the pigeons.

T0322111

BOHUMIL HRABAL

Cutting It Short

Translated by James Naughton

PENGUIN BOOKS

PENGUIN CLASSICS

UK | USA | Canada | Ireland | Australia
India | New Zealand | South Africa

Penguin Books is part of the Penguin Random House group of companies
whose addresses can be found at global.penguinrandomhouse.com.

Penguin
Random House
UK

First published in Czechoslovakia as *Postřižiny* 1976
First published in Great Britain in this translation 1993
Published in Penguin Classics 2017

006

Text copyright © Bohumil Hrabal, 1976
Translation copyright © James Naughton, 1993
Printed and bound in Great Britain by Clays Ltd, Elcograf S.p.A.
The moral rights of the author and translator have been asserted

Set in 10.5/13 pt Dante MT Std
Typeset by Jouve (UK), Milton Keynes

A CIP catalogue record for this book is available from the British Library

ISBN: 978-0-241-29026-2

Cutting It Short

La Bovary, c'est moi

GUSTAVE FLAUBERT

I like those few minutes before seven o'clock at night, when, as a young wife, with rags and a crumpled copy of the newspaper *National Politics*, I clean the glass cylinders of the lamps, with a match I rub off the blackened ends of the burnt wicks, I put the brass caps back, and at seven o'clock precisely that wonderful moment comes when the brewery machinery ceases to function, and the dynamo pumping the electric current around to all the places where the light bulbs shine, the dynamo starts to turn more slowly, and as the electricity weakens, so does the light from the bulbs, slowly the white light grows pink and the pink light grey, filtered through crape and organdie, till the tungsten filaments project red rachitic fingers at the ceiling, a red violin key. Then I light the wick, put on the cylinder, draw out the little yellow tongue of flame, put on the milky shade decorated with porcelain roses. I like those few minutes before seven o'clock in the evening, I like looking upward for those few minutes when the light drains from the bulb like blood from the cut throat of a cock, I like looking at that fading signature of the electric current, and I dread the day the mains will be brought to the brewery and all the brewery lamps, all the airy lamps in the stables, the lamps with round mirrors, all those portly lamps with round wicks one day will cease to be lit, no one will prize their light, for all this ceremonial will be replaced by the light-switch resembling the water tap which replaced the wonderful pumps. I like my burning lamps, in whose light I carry plates and cutlery to the table, open newspapers or books, I like the lamp-lit illumined hands resting just so on the tablecloth, human severed hands, in whose manuscript of wrinkles one may read the character of the one to whom these hands belong, I like the portable paraffin lamps with which I go out of an evening to meet visitors, to shine them in their faces and show them the way, I like the lamps in whose light I crochet curtains and dream deeply, lamps which if extinguished with an abrupt breath emit an acrid smell whose reproach inundates the darkened room. Would that I might find the strength, when the electricity comes to the brewery, to light the lamps at least once a week for one evening and listen to the melodic hissing of the yellow light, which casts deep shadows and compels one into careful locomotion and dreaming.

Francin lit in the office the two portly lamps with their round wicks, two lamps continuously bubbling on like two housekeepers, lamps standing on the edges of a great table, lamps emitting warmth like a stove, lamps sipping paraffin with huge appetite. The green shades of these portly lamps cut off almost with a ruler's edge the areas of light and shadow, so that when I looked in the office window Francin was always split in two, into one Francin soaked in vitriol and another Francin swallowed up in gloom. These tubby brass contraptions, in which the wick was adjusted up or down by a horizontal screw, these brass skeps had a huge draught, so much oxygen did these lamps of Francin's need that they vacuumed up the air around them, so that when Francin placed his cigarette in the vicinity of the lamps the brass hive mouth sucked in ribbons of blue smoke, and the cigarette smoke, as it reached the magic circle of those portly lamps, was mercilessly sucked in and up the draught of the glass cylinder, consumed by the flame, which shone greenishly about the cap like the light given off by a rotted stump of wood, a light like a will-o'-the-wisp, like St Elmo's fire, like the Holy Spirit, which came down in the form of a purple flame hovering over the fat yellow light of the round wick. And Francin entered by the light of these lamps in the outspread brewery books the output of beer, receipts and outgoings, he compiled the weekly and monthly reports, and at the end of every year established the balance for the whole calendar year, and the pages of these books glistened like starched shirt-fronts. When Francin turned the page, these two portly lamps fussed over every motion, threatening to blow out, they squawked, those lamps, as if they were two great birds disturbed out of their sleep, those two lamps positively twitched crossly with their long necks, casting on the ceiling those constantly palpitating shadow-plays of antediluvian beasts, on the ceiling in those half shadows I always saw flapping elephant ears, palpitating rib-cages of skeletons, two great moths impaled on the stake of light ascending from the glass cylinder right up to the ceiling, where over each lamp there shone a round dazzling mirror, a sharply illumined silver coin, which constantly, scarcely perceptibly, but nevertheless shifted about, and expressed the mood of each lamp. Francin, when he turned the page, wrote again the headings with the names and surnames of the public-house landlords. He took a number three lettering pen, and as in the old missals and solemn charters, Francin gave each initial letter in the headings ornaments full of decorative curlicues and billow-ing lines of force, for, when I sat in the office and gazed out of the gloom at his hands, which anointed those office lamps with bleaching-powder, I always had the impression that Francin made those ornamental initials along the lines of my hair, that it gave him the inspiration, he always gave a look at my hair, out of which the light sparkled, I saw in the mirror that wherever I was in the evening, there in my coiffure and the quality of my hair there was always one lamp more. With the lettering pen Francin wrote the basic initial letters, then he took fine pens and as the mood took him dipped them alternately in green and blue and red inks and round the initials began to trace my billowing hair, and like the rose bush growing over and about the arbour, so with the thick netting and branching of the lines of force in my hair Francin orna-mented the initial letters of the names and surnames of the public house landlords.

And when he returned tired from the office, he stood in the doorway in the shadow, the white shirt cuffs showed how he was exhausted by the whole day, these shirt cuffs almost touched his knees, the whole day had placed so many worries and tribulations on Francin's back that he was always ten centimetres shorter, maybe even more. And I knew that the greatest worry was me, that ever since the time he had first seen me, ever since then he had been carrying me in an invisible, and yet all too palpable rucksack on his back, which was growing ever heavier by the day. And then every evening we stood under the burning rise-and-fall lamp, the green shade was so big that there was room for both of us under it, it was a chandelier like an umbrella, under which we stood in the down-pour of hissing light from the paraffin lamp, I hugged Francin with one hand and with the other I stroked the back of his head, his eyes were closed and he breathed deeply, when he had settled down he hugged me at the waist, and so it looked as if we were about to begin some kind of ballroom dance, but in fact it was something more, it was a cleansing bath, in which Francin whispered in my ear everything that had happened to him that day, and I stroked him, and every movement of my hand smoothed away the wrin-kles, then he stroked my loose flowing hair, each time I drew the porcelain chandelier down lower, around the circumference of the chandelier there were thickly hung coloured glass tubes connected by beads, those trinkets tinkled round our ears like spangles and ornaments round the loins of a Turkish dancing girl, sometimes I had the impression that the great adjustable lamp was a glass hat jammed right down over both our ears, a hat hung about with a downpour of trimmed icicles . . . And I expelled the last wrinkle from Francin's face somewhere into his hair or behind his ears, and he opened his eyes, straightened himself up, his cuffs were again at the level of his hips, he looked at me distrustfully, and when I smiled and nodded, he plucked up courage and looked right at me and I at him, and I saw what a great power I had over him, how my eyes entrapped him like the eyes of a striped python when they stare at a frightened finch.

This evening a horse neighed from the darkened yard, then there came another whinny, and then there resounded a thunder-ing of hooves, rattling of chains and jingle of buckles, Francin jerked up and listened, I took a lamp and went out into the passage and opened the door, outside the drayman was calling out in the dark, 'Hey, Ede, Kare, hey whoa!', but no, the two Belgian geldings were pelting away from the stable with a lamp on their breastplate, just as they had returned weary, unharnessed from the dray, in their collars and with the traces hung on the embroidery of those collars and in all their harness after a whole day delivering the beer, just when everyone thought, these gelded stallions can be thinking of nothing else but hay and a pail of draff and a can of oats, so, all of a sudden, four times a year these two geldings recollected their coltish days, their genius of youth, full of as yet undeveloped but nevertheless present glands, and they rose up, they made a little revolt, they gave themselves signals in the gloom of dusks, returning to the stables, and they shied and bolted, but it wasn't shying, they never forgot that still and even up to the last moment even an animal can take the path of freedom . . . and now they flew past the tied houses, on the concrete pavement, under their hooves sparks were kindled like flints, and the lamp on the chest of the offside gelding furiously bucketed about and bobbed and lit up the flitting buckles and broken reins, I leaned forward, and in the tender light of the paraffin lamp that Belgian pair flew past, stout, gigantic geldings, Ede and Kare, who together weighed twenty-five metric quintals, all of which they now put in motion, and that motion constantly threatened to turn into a fall, and the fall of one horse entailed the fall of the other, for they were harnessed together with ties and leather buckles and straps, yet constantly in that gallop they seemed to have a mutual understanding, they bolted simultaneously and alternated in leadership by no more than a couple of centimetres . . . and behind them ran the unfortunate drayman with the whip, the drayman dreading that one of the horses might break its legs, the brewery management would dock it from his pay for years to come . . . and the loss of both horses would mean paying it off till the end of his life . . . 'Hey, Ede and Kare! Hey whoa!', but the team was already dashing into the draught of wind by the maltings, now their hooves softened in the muddy roadway past the chimney and malting floor, the geldings slowed down also, and again by the stables, on the cobble-stones, they speeded up, and on the concrete pavement, illuminated by sharp-edged shafts of light from passages lit by paraffin lamps, on that pavement, drawing hissing sparks from every buckle dragging on the ground, every chain, every hoof, those two Belgians gathered speed, it was no longer a running pace, but a retarded fall, puffs of breath rolled from their nostrils, their eyes were crazed and filled with horror, at the turning by the office both of them skidded on that concrete paving, like a grotesque comedy, but both rode along on their rear hooves, with sparks flying, the drayman stiffened with horror. And Francin rushed to the door, but I stood leaning on the doorpost, praying that nothing would happen to those horses, I knew very well that their incident was also my story too, and Ede and Kare once more in synchrony trotted alongside one another into the draught from the maltings, their hooves grew quiet in the soft mud on the road past the malting floor, and again they gave themselves a signal, and for the third time they flew off, the drayman leapt and the lamp, as one of the horses tugged the bridle, flew in an arc and smashed against the laundry, and the crash of it gave the Belgians new strength, first they neighed one after the other, then both together, and they pelted off along the concrete pavement . . . I looked at Francin, as if it were me who had changed into a pair of Belgian horses, that was my obstinate character, once a month to go crazy, I too suffered a quarterly longing for freedom, I, who was certainly not neutered, but hale and healthy, sometimes a bit too hale and healthy . . . and Francin looked at me, and saw that the bolting Belgian team, those fair blowing manes and powerful air-drawn tails streaming behind their brown bodies, they were me, not me, but my character, my bolting golden coiffure flying through the darkened night, that freely blowing unbound hair of mine . . . and he pushed me aside, and now Francin stood with upraised arms in the tunnel of light flooding from the passage, with uplifted arms he stepped towards the horses and called out, 'Eh-doodoo-doodoo! Whoa!', and the gelded Belgian stallions braked, from beneath their hooves the sparks showered, Francin jumped aside and took the offside horse by the bridle, snatched it and dug it into the foaming maw of the animal, and the motion of the horses ceased, the buckles and reins and straps of the harnessing fell on the ground, the drayman ran up and took the nearside one by the bridle . . . 'Sir, sir . . .' stammered the drayman. 'Wipe them down with straw, and take them through the yard . . . forty thousand crowns that pair cost, do you follow me, Martin?' said Francin, and when he came in the front door like a lancer, and he served with the lancers in the time of Austria, if I hadn't jumped aside he would have knocked me down, he would have stepped right over me . . . and out of the dark came the sound of the whip and the painful whinny of the Belgian horses, swearing and blows with the wrong end of the whip, then the leaping of horses in the dark and cracking of the long whip, wrapping itself round the Belgians' legs and slashing into the skin.

But my portrait is also four pigs, brewery pigs, fed on draff and potatoes, and in the summer, when the beet ripened, I went for the beet leaves and chopped up those leaves and poured yeasty liquid and old beer over them, and the pigs slept twenty hours and put on as much as one kilogram a day, those piggies of mine used to hear me going off to milk the goats, and straightaway they bellowed with joy, because they didn't know that I was going to sell two of them for ham and have two of them slaughtered at home for sausages. As I was milking the goats my porkers would cry out in delight, because they knew that all the milk I got would be poured out right away for them. Mr Cicvárek only glanced at the pigs and said immediately how much those pigs weighed, and always he was right, then he took those two piggies in his arms and threw them into a kind of basketwork gig, a butcher's buggy, drew a net over them and said, 'Those little beggars fight you back just like the old woman the first time I kissed her as a lass.'

Bidding them farewell I said to my piggies, 'Tatty bye, little old piggie-wiggies, you're going to make ever such lovely hams!'

The piggies had no particular desire for such glory, I knew, but all of us have the one death coming to us, and nature is merciful, when there's nothing for it, then everything alive that has to die in a moment, everything is gripped by horror, as if the fuses go, for both man and beast, and then you feel nothing and nothing hurts, that timorousness lowers the wicks in the lamps, till life just dimly flickers and is unaware of anything in its dread. I didn't have much luck with butchers, the first one I had put so much ginger in the sausages that he turned them into confectionery, whereas the second drank so much from first thing in the day that when he lifted the mallet to stun a pig he smashed his own leg, there I was standing with the knife ready, I practically slit that butcher's throat in my fury, then I had to cart him off to the hospital, what's more, and get hold of a replacement. Whereas the third butcher brought his own invention, instead of scalding he had taken to scorching the bristles off with a blow-lamp. I should've junked that butcher in the WC instead of the soup, because for one thing the bristles stayed in the skin, and more important, the pig stank of petrol, so that we had to pour the soup down the drain, because not even the pig that was left would eat it.

Mr Myclík, he was a butcher now, a butcher to my taste. He asked for some marble sponge cake and a white coffee, and had himself a rum, but only once the sausages were in the cauldron, a butcher who brought all his tools wrapped up in napkins, brought with him three aprons, one for slaughtering and scalding and gutting, the other he donned when putting out the offal on the chopping board, and the third apron when everything was almost finished. It was Mr Myclík too who taught me to get one extra spare cauldron and keep that cauldron only for boiling sausages and blood puddings and brawn and offal and heating fat, because whatever cooks in the pan leaves something of itself behind, and a pig-slaughtering, lady, it's the same as a priest serving mass, because, after all, both are a matter of flesh and blood.

And while we baked the bun dough for the sausages and blood puddings, and while we brought the tub, and into the night I boiled the barley and prepared on plates a sufficient quantity of salt and pepper and ginger and marjoram and thyme, the pig had got nothing to eat at midday and began to sense the smell of the butcher's apron, the rest of the livestock too were subdued and quiet, trembling already in advance like aspen leaves, all the other trees are calm and still, the storm is somewhere off in the Carpathians or the Alps, but the aspen leaves tremble and vibrate, like my pig, who is to be slaughtered on the morrow.

I was always the one to go and bring the pig out of the sty. I didn't like them to bind up the piggie's mouth with a rope, why this pain, when I brought the pig treacherously out for the butcher I scratched it on the dewlap, then on the brow, then on its back, and Mr Myclík came from behind with his axe, raised it and knocked down the pig with a mighty blow. For safety's sake he aimed two or three more wet knocks at the pig's splintered skull, I handed Mr Myclík the knife and he knelt down and stuck the blade in its throat, searching a moment for the artery with the point of the blade, and then a gush of blood poured out and I placed the pan beneath, and then another big cauldron. Mr Myclík always, obligingly, while I was changing the containers, stopped up the gushing blood with his hand, then let it go again. Now I had to mix the blood with a wooden whisk to stop it from clotting, then with the other hand too, with both hands simultaneously, I beat at the wonderful smoking blood, Mr Myclík with his helper Mr Martin, the drayman, rolled the pig into the tub and poured boiling water on to it from jugs, and I had to roll up my sleeves and with splayed fingers feel through the cooling blood, take the clotted lumps of blood and throw the stuff to the hens, with both arms up to my elbows in the cooling blood – my arms failed, I waggled them about as if I was on my last legs with the pig, now the last clots of coagulated blood, and the blood settled down, grew cool, I pulled my arms out of the pans and cauldron, while the scalded, shaven pig rose slowly on a crook to the beam of the open shed.

The pig's head lay severed with the dewlap on the board, just then I brought across two shoulders. And now I ran through the yard, my hair tucked under a scarf, so as not to miss a moment, because by now Mr Myclík had rolled out the guts and told his helper to go and turn and wash them, while he himself rummaged in the pig's innards, from memory, like blind Hanuš in the clock, slicing into something else every time, and the spleen and liver and stomach came loose, finally also the lungs and heart. I held the jug ready and all those wonderful lights tumbled out, that symphony of wet colours and shapes, nothing gave me such ecstasy as those pale red pig's lights, wonderfully swollen like crêpe rubber, nothing is so passionate in colouring as the dark brown colour of liver, adorned with the emerald of gall, like clouds before the storm, just like tender cloud fleeces, there running alongside the guts is the knobbly leaf fat, yellow as a guttered candle, as beeswax. And the windpipe too is composed of blue and pale red cartilaginous rings like the suction hose of a coloured vacuum-cleaner. And when we tumbled out that wonderful stuff on to the board, Mr Myclík took a knife, whetted it against a steel, and then sliced off, here a piece of still warm lean meat, here some pieces of liver, here a whole kidney and half a spleen, and I held up a large pan with browned onion and put those pieces of pig straight in the oven, after carefully salting and peppering it all, so that the goulash from the slaughtering would be ready by midday.

Taking a sieve, I strained out the boiled pig's offal, the shoulder, the halved head, turned it on to the board, one piece of meat after another, Mr Myclík removed the bones, and when the meat had cooled a little, I took in my fingers a piece of dewlap and a piece of cheek, instead of bread I chewed some pig's ear, Francin came into the kitchen, he never ate any, he couldn't stomach a thing, so he stood by the stove and had some dry bread and drank some coffee with it, and looked at me and was embarrassed on my behalf, and I ate with relish and drank beer straight from the litre bottle. Mr Myclík smiled, and just for politeness' sake took a bit of meat, but changed his mind and sipped his white coffee and tasted his marble cake, then he took his mincing knife, rolled up his sleeves, and with powerful motions of the knife the lumps of meat began to lose their shape and function, and with the half-moon slicings of the rocker blades the meat gradually became sausage-meat. And Mr Myclík proffered his palm, and I poured scalded spices into it, Mr Myclík was the one butcher whose spices I had to drench first in boiling water, because, he said, and I understood him quite palpably, it makes for a greater dispersion and delicacy of aroma. And then he added the soaked bread-roll crumb and again mixed it all thoroughly and ran through it with his powerful hands and fingers and mixed it through and through, then he tugged the sausage-meat off both his hands, dug into it, tried it for taste, gazed at the ceiling, and at that moment was as handsome as a poet, he stared at the ceiling in delight, repeating over to himself: pepper, salt, ginger, thyme, bread-roll, garlic, and as he pattered over that quick-fire butcher's tiny prayer, he dug into the sausage-meat and offered me some. I took it on my finger and put it in my mouth and tasted it, staring likewise at the ceiling, and with eyes brimful with piggy delight I unfurled and relished on my tongue the peacock fantail of all those aromas, and then I nodded my assent, that as the mother of the household I approved of this gamut of flavours, and nothing now stood in the way of getting down to making the sausages themselves. And so Mr Myclík took the trimmed skins, spaled with a splint at one end, with two fingers of the right hand he parted the aperture and with the other hand just stuffed, and out of his fist there grew a wonderful sausage, which I took and fastened with a spale, and so we worked, and all the while as the sausage-meat declined, so in their jointed vessels of skins the heap of sausages rose.

'Mr Martin, where have you got to again?' Mr Myclík called out every other while, and every time this Mr Martin, the drayman, maybe all the days of his life, whenever he had a moment, he had loitered, in the shed, in the stable, behind the cart, in the passageways, he drew out a little round mirror and looked at himself, he was so enamoured of himself, he was always overpowered by whatever it was he saw in that little round mirror, for hours on end he could linger in the stable, forgetting to go home, all because he was plucking bristles from his nose with the tweezers, plucking hairs from his eyebrows, he even dyed not only his hair, but even coloured his eye-lashes and powdered his face. I'd tell myself, next time Francin would have to get me another helper from the brewery. 'Mr Martin, for Christ's sake where have you got to again? Slice up this gut fat, we're going to make barley and breadcrumb puddings, where have you been?'

Mr Myclík loaded the barley puddings, by now he'd drunk his second pouring of rum, then, quite out of the blue, he just dug into the blood-soaked sausage-meat and smeared a bloody smudge on my face with his finger. And quietly he started to laugh, his eye glinting like a ring, I dipped into the bloody pan myself, and when I tried to smear the butcher one on the face he ducked aside and I planted my palm on the white wall, but before I'd wiped it off Mr Myclík had given me another smudge, then he carried on skewering the pudding. I dipped into the blood again and made a dash at him, Mr Myclík ducked me several times like a Savoy medley, then I smeared his face with blood, and went on skewering the barley puddings, and laughed when I saw the butcher laughing with his great hearty laughter, it wasn't just any old laughter, it was a laughter from somewhere way back out of pagan times, when people believed in the force of blood and spittle. I couldn't resist scooping up some barley blood and smearing it again in Mr Myclík's face, and he ducked me again, I missed him, and with a great big chuckle he planted me another smudge, and carried on skewering the puddings. Mr Martin brought a crate of beer over from the bottling room, and as he bent down carefully I smeared him in the face with a full palm of bloody sausage-meat, and Mr Martin the drayman drew his little round mirror out of his pocket, looked at himself, and probably he was even more enamoured of himself than usual, he gave a hearty laugh and scooped up three fingerfuls of red sausage-meat. I dashed into the living room, Mr Martin ran after me, I shouted out, not even realizing that behind the wall the brewery management board was in session, you could distinctly hear the scraping of chairs and calling of voices, but Mr Martin besmirched me with blood and laughed, the blood brought us closer together somehow, I laughed and sat myself down on the sofa, holding my hands out in front of me like a puppet, so as not to mess up the covers, Mr Martin likewise held his messy hand up in the same gesture, while the rest of his whole body gradually dissolved with laughter, shook, and his throat burst into a choking, jubilant, coughing chuckle. And Mr Myclík dashed up and scooped with a full palm at Mr Martin's face, the barley grains glistened in it like pearls, and Mr Martin stopped laughing, he went solemn, it seemed as if he wanted to hit someone, but he only drew out his little round pocket mirror, looked at himself in it, and seemingly found himself even better looking than he had ever seen himself before, and he guffawed with laughter, opening wide the sluice gates of his throat and bellowing with laughter, and Mr Myclík, an interval of a third lower, chuckled away with a small-scale laughter which matched the little teeth under his black moustache, and so we roared together with laughter and didn't know why, one look was enough and off we went, bursting into stitches of mirth which hurt in the side. And now the door opened and in rushed Francin in his frock coat, pressing his cabbage-leaf-shaped tie against his chest, and when he saw the blood-smeared faces and the terrible laughter, he clasped his hands, but I couldn't restrain myself, I took three fingers of bloody sausage-meat and smeared Francin in the face, to make him laugh in spite of himself, but he took such fright that he ran, just as he was, into the boardroom, two members of the board of management collapsed on the spot, because they thought a crime had been committed in the brewery. Doctor Gruntorád himself, the chairman, ran by the back entrance into the kitchen, looked about him, and when he saw that broad laughter on the blood-smeared faces he sighed a sigh of relief, sat himself down, and I, with my hands messy with sausage-meat, made a red stripe on the doctor's face, and for just a moment we all went quiet, gazing through tearful eyes at our chairman Dr Gruntorád, who rose to his feet and clenched his fists and thrust out his bulldog jaw . . . but all of a sudden he bayed with laughter, it was that force of blood, that sacral something which, in order to be averted, was discharged from time immemorial by this smearing with pig's blood, the doctor dug into the sausage-meat and rushed at me, I ran laughing into the living room, the doctor missed me and landed his hand on the ready made-up bed, he went into the kitchen and scooped up a fistful and returned, I ran round the table, the white cloth was full of my palm prints, every other moment Dr Gruntorád dotted the tablecloth with blood, he headed me off and I ran squealing into the passage connecting our flat with the boardroom, the lights were on in the room and I ran into the meeting, golden chandeliers and beneath them a long table covered with green baize, upon which files and reports lay outspread. And Gruntorád, chairman of the board, rushed in after me, all the members of the management board thought their chairman was after my blood, that he'd tried to kill me already. Francin sat on a chair and mopped his brow with a bloodstained hand, and the chairman chased me several times round the table, I shrieked and the sweat poured from both of us, when suddenly my foot slipped and I fell, and Doctor Gruntorád, chairman of the municipal brewery, and limited-liability company, splodged a full hand in my face and sat down, his cuffs drooped and he started to laugh, he laughed just like me, we laughed together, but that laughter only enhanced the consternation of the members of the management board, because they all thought we had gone quite dotty.

'Gentlemen, if I may be so bold, I invite you all to our slaughtering party,' I said.

And Dr Gruntorád declared:

'Manager, have ten crates of bottled lager brought over from the plant. No no, make it twelve!'

'Come along, this way, gentlemen, if you please, but you'll have to eat the pork goulash with a spoon from a soup bowl, right up to the brim! And in a little bit we'll have sausages too with horseradish, and barley and breadcrumb puddings. Gentlemen, come this way please,' with a motion of my blood-spattered hand I invited my guests in by the rear entrance.

It was late at night when the members of the management board dispersed to go home in their buggies. I accompanied each with a lamp in my hand, the vehicles drove up in front of the entrance, glowing carriage lamps fitted on mudguards illuminated the dimly gleaming hindquarters of horses, all the members of the management board squeezed Francin's hand and clapped him on the shoulder. That night I slept alone in the bedroom, cold air streamed in through the open window, on planks between chairs the sausages and puddings glittered on their rye straw, right by the bed on long boards lay cooling the dismembered parts of the pig, the boned and apportioned hams, the chops and roasting joints, the shoulders and knees and legs, all laid out according to Mr Myclík's orderly system. As I got into bed I could hear Francin in the kitchen getting up and pouring himself some lukewarm coffee, taking some dry bread to chew with it, it had been a tremendous blow-out, all the members of the management board ate abundantly, only

Francin stood there in the kitchen drinking lukewarm coffee and chewing dry bread with it. I lay in the feather quilt, and before I fell asleep, I stretched out a hand and touched a shoulder, then I fingered a joint and went dozing off with my fingers on a virginal tenderloin, and dreamed of eating a whole pig. When towards morning I woke, I had such a thirst, I went barefoot to fetch a bottle of beer, pulled off the stopper and drank greedily, then I lit the lamp, and holding it in my fingers, I went from one bit of pork to the next, unable to restrain myself from lighting the primus and slicing off two lovely lean schnitzels from the leg. I beat them out thin, salted and peppered them and cooked them in butter in eight minutes flat, all that time, which seemed to me an eternity, my mouth was watering, that was what I needed, to eat practically the whole of the two legs, in simple unbreaded schnitzels sprinkled with lemon juice. I added some water to the schnitzels, covered the pan with a lid, out of which angry steam huffed and puffed, and now I laid those schnitzels on a plate and ate them greedily, as always I got my nightdress spattered, just as I always spatter my blouse with juice or gravy, because when I eat, I don't just eat, I guzzle . . . and when I had finished and wiped the plate with bread, I saw through the open door how, there in the twilight gloom, Francin's eyes were staring, just those eyes reproaching me again for eating as ill becomes a decent woman, and it was as well I had eaten my fill already, for that look of his always spoilt my appetite, I bent over the lamp, but then I remembered the reek of the wick would affect the flavour of the meat, I carried the lamp into the passage and blew it out with a powerful puff of breath. And so I climbed into bed, and feeling the shoulder of pork, dropped off to sleep, looking forward in the morning when I woke to making two more plain schnitzels.

3

Bod'a Červinka always took great pains with my hair. He said, 'That hair of yours is a hark back to the golden days of yore, never have I had such hair under my comb before.' When Bod'a combed out my hair, it was as if he had lit two burning torches in the shop, there in the mirrors and bowls and glass bottles the fire of my hair blazed up, and I had to admit that Bod'a was right. Never did I see my hair look so beautiful elsewhere as it did in Bod'a's shop, when he washed it in camomile infusion, which I boiled myself and brought along in a milk can. While my hair was still wet it never had the promise of what began to happen to it when it dried out; the moment it started to dry it was as if in those streaming tresses thousands of golden bees were born, thousands of little tiny fire-flies, the crackling of thousands of little tiny amber crystals. And when Bod'a first drew the comb through this mane of tresses, there came a crackling and a hissing from them, and they swelled and grew and seethed, till Bod'a had to kneel down, as if he were grooming the tails of a couple of stallions with a currycomb. And his shop was illuminated with it, cyclists jumped off their bikes and pressed their faces to the window to confirm and explain what had so startled their eyes. And Bod'a himself dwelt in the cloudy expanse of my hair, he always locked and closed the shop so as not to be disturbed, every now and again he sniffed at the scent of it, and when he had finished combing he breathed out blissfully, and only then did he bind the hair, just as the mood, which I trusted, took him, sometimes with a purple, at other times a green, or else a red or a blue ribbon, as if I was part of a Catholic rite, as if my hair was part of some feast of the church. Then he unlocked the shop, brought me my bicycle, hung the can on the frame, and helped me ceremoniously up on to the saddle. By then there was a crowd of people in front of the shop, everyone stared at that hair smelling sweetly of camomile. When I leant on the pedals Mr Bod'a ran alongside for a bit and held up my hair to prevent it from catching in the chain or the spokes. And when I had got up enough speed Mr Bod'a tossed up a corner of my tresses in the air, as you would throw up in the air a star or a kite up into the sky, and breathless he returned to the shop. And I rode off, and as my hair blew behind me, I could hear its crackling, like someone rubbing salt or silk, like when rain trickles off down a tin roof, like Wiener schnitzel frying, so that torch of tresses blew behind me, as when boys at dusk with burning pitch broomsticks run about on the Mayday night of Philip and James or burn witches, so the smoke of my hair blew behind me. And people stopped, and I wasn't surprised that they couldn't tear themselves away from that blowing hair as it came and accosted them like an advertisement. And I felt good myself when I saw how I was seen, the empty can of camomile jangled on the handlebars and the comb of streaming air swept my hair back. I rode through the square, all glances converging on my flowing tresses like spokes on the wheels of this bicycle on which my moving Ego trod the pedals. Francin met me twice flowing along like this, and each time this blowing hair of mine took his breath away, he didn't even acknowledge my presence, he was quite incapable of calling out to me, he just stood there numbed by my unexpected apparition, pressing himself to the wall and obliged to pause a moment to get his breath back. I had the feeling he would have keeled over if I had spoken to him, it was his loving adoration which pressed him to the wall, like the picture by Aleš of the orphan child in all the school readers. And I trod on the pedals, knocking my knees alternately against the can, cyclists riding the other way halted, some turned their bikes and sped after me, overtook me, only to turn their bicycles round and ride again to meet me, and they greeted my little blouse and milk can and my blowing hair and me in my entirety, and affably and understandingly I granted them this show and only regretted I did not have the ability to ride to meet myself like this one day, so that I could also take pleasure in what I took pride in and could not be ashamed of. I rode once more through the square, and then up the main thoroughfare, there stood the Orion motorcycle in front of the Grand, in front of it Francin holding a spark plug in his fingers, there he stood with that motorbike of his, and certainly he saw me, but he pretended not to, his Orion was always playing up with its ignition and whatnot, so that Francin carried always in the sidecar with him not only all his spanners and wrenches and screwdrivers, but also a little treadle lathe. And next to Francin stood two members of the management board of our limited-liability brewery. Before slapping my shoe on the pavement I reached behind me and drew my hair forward, and laid it in my lap.

'Hello, Francin,' I said.

And Francin blew into the spark plug, but when he heard me the spark plug dropped from his fingers, his face had two smudges on it from the repairing.

'Good day to you,' the two management board members greeted me.

'Good morning, lovely weather, isn't it?' I said, and Francin blushed to the roots of his hair.

'Where have you dropped that spark plug, Francin?' I said.

And I bent down, Francin knelt and searched for the spark plug under the sidecar, I laid a little hankie on the pavement, knelt down and my hair fell beside me, Mr de Giorgi, master chimneysweep, took up my hair tenderly and threw it across his elbow, like a sacristan taking a priest's robe, Francin kneeled and fixed his eyes under the blue shadow of the motorcycle sidecar, and I saw that my presence had so disconcerted him that he was searching only in order to regain his composure. When we had our wedding it was the same thing again, as he was putting the ring on me his fingers trembled so much that the wedding ring dropped out and rolled away somewhere, and so first Francin, then the witnesses, then the wedding guests, first bending over, then on all fours, and finally the priest himself, all of them were crawling on all fours about the church, until the server found that wedding ring under the pulpit, a little round ring that had rolled off quite the opposite way to where the whole wedding had been searching, down on its hands and knees. And I laughed that day, I just stood there and I laughed . . .

'There's something over there by the gutter,' a child said, passing by and bowling his hoop on down the main street.

And there by the gutter the spark plug lay, Francin picked it up in his fingers, and when he tried to screw it into the engine his hands shook so much that the spark plug chattered in the threads. And the doors of the Grand opened and out came Mr Bernádek, master blacksmith, who drank a keg of Pilsner at a sitting, and he carried out a glass of beer.

'Come on, young missus, don't be shy, have one on me!'

'Cheers, Mr Bernádek!'

I sank my nose in the foam, raised my arm as if to take the oath, and slowly and with relish I drank down that sweetly bitter liquid, and when I had emptied the glass, I wiped my lips with my forefinger and said, 'But our own brewery beer is just as good.'

Mr Bernádek gave me a bow:

'But the Pilsner beer, young missus, is nearer to the colour of your hair, allow me . . .' mumbled the master blacksmith, 'allow me to go back in and continue drinking in your honour some more of that golden hair of yours.'

He bowed and left, a presence that weighed a hundred and twenty kilos, and whose trousers made huge flaps at the back, flaps like those of an elephant.

'Francin,' I said, 'are you coming back for your dinner?'

He tightened the spark plug at the top of the engine, feigning concentration. I bowed to the two honourable members of the management board, trod on the pedals, tossed behind me those streaming tresses of Pilsner, and gaining speed rode off down the narrow lane on to the bridge, and the land beyond the balustrade unfurled in front of me like an umbrella. You could smell the scent of the river, and there in the distance rose the beige-walled brewery with its maltings, our limited-liability company municipal brewery.

4

On the lid of the muscle builder box was the message: You too shall possess the same fine physique, powerful muscles and stunning strength!

And every morning Francin would exercise his muscles, which were just as magnificent as the gladiator's on the box lid anyway, but Francin saw himself as just a puny little skinned rabbit. I put the pot of potatoes on the stove, took the box with the photo of the great muscle-man on the lid, and read out loud:

'You too shall have the strength of a tiger that with one blow of its paw kills prey much larger than itself.'

At that moment Francin glanced out to the pavement, and the muscle builder withered in his fingers, and Francin straightaway collapsed on the ottoman in a heap and said, 'Pepin.'

'Now at last I'm going to see that brother of yours, at long last I'm going to hear something from my little old brother-in-law!'

And I leant against the window frame, and there on the pavement stood a man, with a small oval hat on his head, wearing check breeches tucked into green Tyrolean stockings, with an upturned nose and on his back an army rucksack.

'Uncle Jožin,' I called out to him from the doorstep, 'come on in.'

'Which one are you?' asked Uncle Pepin.

'Your sister-in-law, you're right welcome!'

'Christ, I'm a lucky lad, to have such a fine winsome sister-in-law, but what've you done with Francin?' Uncle enquired, rolling on into the kitchen and living-room.

'Here he is, but what's up with the man? Lying down are you? Good God, man, I've come to pay you a visit, I won't be staying more than a fortnight,' Uncle ran on and his voice boomed and sliced the air like an army banner, like a military command, and Francin felt an electric shock hit him with each word, and he leapt up and wrapped himself in a blanket.

'All of them sends their love, except Bóchalena, she's a goner, some joker put gunpowder in her woodpile, when the old thing popped a log on the stove, it went off, lammed her right in the mug, and that was that, she just snuffed it.'

'Bóchalena?' I clasped my hands: 'Your sister?'

'Sister? No. Local woman, old girl that crammed herself all day with apples and buns, for thirty years she'd always be saying, "Oh, you young folks, I'll be gone soon, I dinna want to do nothing, just sleep . . ." me neither, I'm no exactly one hundred per cent,' said Uncle, untying the cords of his haversack and tumbling all his cobbler's tools out on the floor, and Francin, hearing the clatter, covered his face with his hands and groaned, as if Uncle had tumbled all that shoemaker's equipment out into his brains.

'Uncle Jožin,' I said, shoving the baking tin in front of his face, 'have yourself a bun.'

And Uncle Pepin ate two buns, and declared, 'I'm really no a hundred per cent.'

'Surely no,' I fell on my knees and clasped my hands over those lasts and hammers and leather-cutting knives and other cobbler's bits and pieces.

'You just watch it!' Uncle Pepin cried with alarm. 'Dinna go and mess it up with that hair of yours, but listen Francin lad, Zbořil the priest's broke his leg at the hip sae bad he'll just be a cripple for life. Uncle Zavičák, he was up doing the roof of the church tower when the cradle slipped and him with it and down he went, but he grabs a hold of the hand of the clock, and there he is, holding on to this hand on the tower clock, but the hand shifts, it slips from a quarter past eleven right down to half past, and so, as Uncle goes hurtling, his hands lose their grip on the clock hand and he just plummets, but there's lime trees growing down there, so Uncle plonks into the top of one of they, and Zbořil the vicar, as he just stands there watching, he's wringing his hands to see Zavičák drop from branch to branch, and then he falls on his back on the ground, and Zbořil comes rushing over to congratulate him, but he overlooks this step, see, he falls and breaks his leg, so old Zavičák has to load up Zbořil the minister, and off they cart him to the hospital in Prostějov.'

I picked up a wooden last for a lady's shoe and stroked it.

'These are really lovely things, aren't they, Francin?' I said, but Francin groaned, as if I was showing him a rat or a frog.

'Aye they're right beauties,' said Uncle and pulled out his pince-nez, placed it on his nose, and there were no lenses in the pince-nez, and Francin, when he saw that lensless pince-nez on his brother's nose, he whimpered, he almost wept and turned to the wall, then he tossed about and the springs of the sofa moaned just like Francin.

'And what's our Uncle over in the Great Lakes doing?' I asked.

Uncle gave a dismissive wave of the hand, and took Francin by the shoulder and turned him round to face him, and related to him in a great voice full of glee:

'Well now, Uncle Metud over in the Great Lakes he's begun to get a wee bit strange, and one day he read a notice in the paper: Suffer from boredom? Get yourself a racoon. And Uncle Metud, what with having no kids and that, he replied to the ad, and in a week's time the beast arrived, in a packing case. Well that was a thing now! Just like a child, it made friends with anybody going, but there was one special thing about it, you see, the German for racoon is *Waschbär*, and whatever that racoon saw, it simply had to wash it, and so it washed Uncle Metud's alarm clock and three watches, till nobody could put them together again. Then one day it washed all the spices. And again, when Uncle Metud took his bicycle to pieces, the racoon went and washed the parts for him in the nearest creek, and the neighbours were coming along saying: Uncle Metud, would you be needing this piece of junk at all? We just found it over in the creek! And after they'd brought him several bits like that, Metud went to have a look himself, and that racoon had gone off with practically the whole bang shoot. My those buns are good though. And that racoon he would only do his business in the wardrobe, so the

whole building stank of his pee, in the end they had to lock everything up from him, they even had to start whispering when they
spoke together. My those buns are good, pity I'm no one hundred
per cent. But the racoon kept watching to see where they put the
key, it went and unlocked whatever they were keeping from him.
But the worst of it was, the animal kept a look-out in the evenings,
and soon as Uncle Metud gave Auntie a wee kiss, the racoon went
for him and wanted to have some too, so Uncle Metud had to go
down to the woods wi' Auntie Rozára courting like before they
were married, and still they had to keep turning round in case the
racoon was right there behind them. And so there was no time for
boredom, till once they went off for two days and the racoon was
sae bored that this one Whitsun holiday he dismantled the whole
big tiled stove in the living room, made such a muck of the furnish-
ings and the feather quilt and the linen in the commode, that Uncle
Metud sat down and wrote him an ad to *The Moravian Eagle*: Suffer
from boredom? Get yourself a racoon! And ever since then he's been
cured of his melancholia.'

Uncle Pepin went on, and as he talked he ate one bun after
another, and now he felt into the baking tin, he fingered the whole
baking tin, and finding it empty he waved a hand and said:

'I'm no quite one hundred per cent.'

'Like Bóchalena,' I said.

'What nonsense are you blethering?' Uncle Pepin broke into a
shout: 'Bóchalena was just a poor old thing that crammed herself
with apples, except she also had visions . . .'

'Was it the apples?' I interrupted.

'Bollocks! Visions, these old lassies get visions, she got it from
the church,' Uncle Pepin said choking, 'a great big horse flying in
the night over our wee town, and the mane and tail of that horse
blazing with fire, well and as Bóchalena said at the time, "It'll be
war," and it was war too, but Francin lad, last year the whole town
was in a right tizz! The old women were falling down on their
knees, I saw it too, over the square and over the church, this baby
Jesus figure flying through the air! But then it all came out, that
tootsy wee chappie Lolan had been out watching his lambs, and the

airyplanes exercising overhead, lugging after them some kind of punchbag and potting at it with their popguns, they clean forgot about the rope, you see, and as it dangled along the ground, so it got tangled up all round Lolan's leg, and him a braw wee child too, with his dainty fair hair, and as the airyplane flew upwards, the rope went up and Lolan with it, and right over our wee town Lolan went, flying through the air, but the old women they thought it was baby Jesus, specially when the rope got hooked up on a lime tree by the church, and this baby Jesus fell down like Uncle Zavičák, tumbling from branch to branch, and then wee Lolan falls to earth and says "Where are all my poor wee lambs?" and the old women knelt down for him to bless them.'

So Uncle continued, and his voice was resounding and triumphant and blared right through the room.

Francin got dressed, pulled on his coat, his frock coat, tied with his fingers his tie shaped like a cabbage leaf, I adjusted his gutta-percha collar with folded-down corners, raised my eyes and gazed into his, and gave him a little peck on the tip of his finger.

'A fortnight?' he whispered. 'You'll see, he'll stay a fortnight right enough, and maybe just the rest of his life!'

When I saw how unhappy he was, I planted a proper kiss on his lips, and he was embarrassed, he looked at me reproachfully, a decent woman doesn't behave like this in public, even though the only public present was actually Uncle Pepin, and Francin extracted himself from my embrace and went off through the back entrance to the office. Through the wall I heard the glazed swing doors burst open, ah, Francin and his 'decent behaved woman', ever since I married him, he's been raising the matter, raising the spectre of this decent woman, sketching out the pattern of his model woman, which I never was and never could be, I that so much loved eating cherries, but when I ate them my way, greedily and ravenously, he reddened to the roots of his hair, and I couldn't fathom the cause of his annoyance, until I saw for myself, that a cherry held in my lips was indeed a reason for his discomfiture, because a decent woman simply doesn't eat cherries quite so greedily as that. When in the autumn I scrubbed the heads of corn on the cob, again he looked at my scrubbing palm and the tiny glints of fire in my eyes, and there again, a decent woman just doesn't scrub corn on the cob quite like that, and if she does, well not with such great laughter and flaming eyes as mine, if some male stranger were to see this, he might see in my hands scrubbing that corn on the cob some sort of a sign favourable to his hankerings.

Uncle Pepin laid out his precious cobbler's treasure on a little stool, then he took off my shoe, and elaborating to me on all its parts, he replaced his lensless pince-nez and said to me grandly:

'And since you're a lady of such outstanding intellectuality, I'm going to mend you all your broken shoes, because I've made foot-wear for the official supplier by appointment to the court, that was patronized not only by the imperial court, but all throughout the world, that delivered shoes . . .'

'By bicycle,' said I.

'Bollocks!' roared Uncle Pepin. 'Do you think your court sup-plier is just the same as your common or garden rat-catcher, or peltmonger? He delivers by ship and by rail, if the Emperor ever met his sort riding on a bicycle . . .'

'Did the Emperor ride a bicycle too?' I clasped my hands.

'What are you twittering on about, you twittering magpie?' Uncle shouted. 'I'm telling you, if the Emperor met the likes of your court-appointed supplier riding on a bicycle he'd have taken his . . .'

'Bicycle off him,' I said.

'Bollocks! Taken his court appointment off him and the eagle out of his crest!' Uncle Pepin choked and spluttered, but then, tak-ing a look at the stool, he gave a blissful grin, took out a pot, opened it, sniffed and gave it to me to sniff too and waved his hand:

'Feast your eyes on this, sister-in-law, it's cobbler's glue alias shoe-maker's gum,' said Uncle Pepin, placing the open pot on a chair.

Through the wall you could hear the rattling of chairs in the boardroom, subdued conversation, the shuffling of heels, then the chairs went silent and Francin opened the meeting in a quiet voice with a report on the state of the brewery over the past month.

'Uncle Jožin,' I ventured, 'so this man really supplied shoes to the court and the estates?'

'Bollocks!' roared Uncle Pepin. 'What are you twittering on about like a silly bairn? What's a court supplier got to do with farming and cattle-estates? A court supplier's a pretty touchy character, now old Kafka, he was that touchy, always on edge, once when his wee daughter kept bashing her head on every sharp edge of furniture, old Kafka, that court supplier by appointment, he took a whole basketful of shoulder pads out from the workshop and he stuck a pad on every single corner of the furniture, but then what with him being so mighty on edge, he went and flung the door open that sharp, he knocked his wee lassie right out with the door, so Látal now, he advised him just to put another pad on his daughter's forrid.'

'Látal, would that be Francin's cousin, Uncle Jožin?' I said.

'Balls!' Uncle Pepin cried. 'Látal the school-teacher! Last year he fell out of a first floor classroom right in the middle of demonstrating uniform time and motion . . . like it's when a train just keeps chugging along and along and along and along and along . . . and Látal struck out with both arms flailing and like a train he pounded along over to the open window, and then he fell right out the window, and the whole class rushed gleefully to the window, surely teacher must've broken both his legs in the tulip bed, but Látal wasna there, he'd cut round the yard and nipped up the stair, and again, there his train was, chugging along and along and along . . . and in he came to the classroom, behind the backs of the schoolkids that was still leaning out of the window.'

In the boardroom through the wall you could hear the voice of the chairman, Doctor Gruntorád:

'Manager, who's making that infernal roar out there?'

'Sorry, sir, my brother's here on a visit,' said Francin.

'Well, Manager, just you go and tell your brother from us to pipe down! This is our brewery!'

'Now that Látal fellow's wife was Mercina, your cousin, wasn't she, Uncle Jožin?' I said doucely.

'Not a bit of it! Mercina's the one married Uncle Vaňura, chef on the Balkan express, ye know, lived in Bohemia, hereabouts, somewhere in Mnichovo Hradiště, and when that Balkan express went through Mnichovo Hradiště once a week regular, Mercina used to let the dog out every time at half ten, it went down to the station, Uncle Vaňura leant out of the Balkan express and dropped it a muckle parcel of bones, and the dog took it off home, but one day this year, when Vaňura let go the bones, the parcel went and clobbered the stationmaster one, and old Vaňura had to pay for fouling up his uniform!' Uncle Pepin hollered on.

And again he picked up my shoe and put on that lensless pince-nez and roared out radiantly, 'But never you heed this nonsense, I'll explain it you once all over again, then I'll hand it to you to have a try! So this here is Pariser Schnitt, and this is the vamp or *Gelenk*, alias ankle upper. This here is the sole, alias bottom leather, and this is your heel or *Absatz*. Mind you, sister-in-law, anyone that wants to be a shoemaker or a cobbler has to have a certificate of apprenticeship, and that's like getting your school leaving certificate or a college doctorate. Now that court-supplier Weinlich . . .'

'Ulrich?' I said, cupping my ear with my hand.

'Weinlich!' roared Uncle. 'Wein as in wine, there's this idiot scuffs up his shoes and brings them to this court-supplier chappie Weinlich and the supplier says: "Good God man, these shoes are wrecked, what am I supposed to do with them?" And the idiot says, "Sell 'em to the Jews." Now Weinlich was Jewish himself, and he starts roaring, "So Jews are swine, are they?"'

'Peps,' I said softly.

'Balls!' thundered Uncle, rearing threateningly over me. 'I've had nothing but glowing testimonials, and what would a fancy gent like that be associating with me for! What d'ye mean, Peps? Sister-in-law, you're as daft as in a school test afore noon!'

And Uncle gave himself such a clout on the brow with his fist that his pince-nez flew under the cabinet, but one glance at my shoe simmered him down, he seated himself and pointing with his fingertip continued with his vociferous schooling:

'And this as we've said already's the *Absatz* or heel, and on that heel or *Absatz* there's the heel-piece, heel-tap, and edge-piece otherwise known amongst the footwear profession as the rand!'

I picked up a long iron spoon, whose end was as rough as an ox's tongue, and I said, 'Uncle Jožin, this is the *Abnehmer*, isn't it?'

'What?' Uncle roared woundedly. 'The *Abnehmer* is this thing here, *Abnehmer* alias remover, but the thing you're got in your hand is a rasp or a file or a scraper!'

And the door flew open, and in the doorway stood Francin, pressing his tie down with his palm, he spread out his arms and bent his knees, he bowed to Uncle Jožin and then to me, bowed to the waist and said:

'You two uhlans, what are you yelling away like that for? Jožko, why all the howling?' and he put his hand in the open pot of gum.

'It's no me,' mumbled Uncle Pepin.

'Who is it then? Is it . . . me for instance?' Francin pointed to himself with both hands.

'It's somebody in here, inside of me,' said Uncle Pepin, knitting and twisting his fingers with embarrassment.

'Cool down, the brewery management board is meeting, the chairman himself sent me to give you the message,' Francin raised his hand and retreated into the passage . . .

Then you could hear Francin's quiet voice again, carrying on with his report, in which he explained how the debits for the month which had just expired would be evened out by the proceeds of the month to come. I brought over a pot of pork dripping and spread slice after slice of bread for Uncle Pepin, each time as he was about to speak I handed him another slice, but through in the boardroom Francin's voice came to a halt, you heard the shuffling of heels, then exclamations, the legs of the Thonet chairs rattled, as if all the members of the management board had risen to their feet, I thought it must be the end of the meeting, but the voice of the chairman of the brewery management board, Doctor Gruntorád, boomed out: 'Meeting adjourned for ten minutes!'

The door connecting the office with the passage flew open as if with a kick, and into the room rushed Francin, pressing his hand to his tie and shouting:

'Who put that glue on the chair there for me? Crivens! I've got one sheet of paper stuck down so hard I couldn't even turn the page! Mr de Giorgi tried to help and he got so messed up he couldn't even get his hands off the green baize! And the chairman's got it on his pince-nez, it's stuck fast to his nose! And my fingers, what's more, have stuck to my tie, look at me!' Francin pulled away his hand and the elastic bands holding his tie went taut.

'I'll bring you a bit of warm water,' I said.

But Francin jerked his hand forward abruptly and the elastic bands stretched and burst, and the hand with the tie shot forward while the elastic bands jabbed Francin in the neck, and he moaned softly like a little boy: 'Oooh!'

Uncle Pepin took the lid off the pot, presented it to Francin and announced proudly:

'This stuff is manufactured by that Mecca of the footwear world, the Vienna firm of Salamander and Co.!'

And Uncle held up his lensless pince-nez to his nose.

5

Every month Francin went to Prague on his motorcycle, but every time something broke down, so he had to mend it. All the same he would return radiant, handsome, and I always had to hear down to the last detail all the things he had had to do to make his unroadworthy Orion into a motorcycle again, one that always made it to its destination. Made it means that the motorcycle got back to the brewery, even though sometimes he had to push it the last stretch. But he never cursed and swore, he would push the whole contraption ten, fifteen, or maybe only five kilometres, and when he pushed the Orion in from Zvěřínek, a village three kilometres away, Francin enthused about how much better it was getting. Today Francin returned from Prague pulled by a yoke of bullocks. When he had paid the farmer he rushed into the kitchen, and as always I gave him a hug, we stepped again under the rise-and-fall lamp, and anybody peeping in the window would have had to wonder. For when Francin returned from Prague, each time there was this particular ritual, Francin shut his eyes and I reached into his breast pocket, but Francin shook his head, and then I unbuttoned his coat and reached into his waistcoat pocket, and Francin still shook his head, and then I reached into his trouser pocket and Francin nodded his head, and all the while he kept his eyes blissfully closed, and always I drew out of some place of concealment in his clothing a little tiny parcel, and out of that parcel, which I slowly unwrapped, feigning astonished surprise and delight, I unpacked a little ring, sometimes a brooch, once a wristwatch even. But this ritual was not the first, before, when Francin returned from Prague, where he went once a month to visit Brewers House, when he came in, he always waited till it was getting dark, told me to shut my eyes, and I used to shut my eyes the minute he came into the kitchen, Francin led me off to the living room, sat me in front of the mirror and made me promise I wouldn't look, and when I promised, he put a wonderful hat on my head, and Francin said, 'Now,' and I looked into the mirror and took that hat in my fingers and adjusted it to my own taste, then turned round and Francin enquired of me, 'Who was it bought you this, Maryška?' and I said, 'Francin,' and kissed him on the hand and he stroked me. And other times he brought me something which he put round my neck and which chilled me, and I opened my eyes, and there in the mirror was glittering a necklace, a piece of Jablonec jewellery, and Francin would ask me, 'Who was it bought you this?' And I kissed him on the hand and said, 'You, Francin.' And then he asked, 'And who is this Francin?' And I said: 'My little hubby.' And so every month I got some present or other, Francin had all my body measurements, he knew them off by heart, he always used to ask me casually, in advance, what might I possibly like to have? And I never said it out straight, I always chatted on about something and Francin got the message. And then, the first time he brought me a ring, he stepped under the rise-and-fall lamp and taught me for the first time to search through his pockets, greater and lesser, and I always guessed where the present probably was, but always I went for that place last, to make Francin happy.

Today, when he returned drawn by the yoke of bullocks, he asked me to shut my eyes. And he carried something through into the living room. And then he put the light out in the living room and took me by the hand and led me through with closed eyes, he sat me down on the little armchair in front of the mirror, then he went and drew the curtains. I heard the lid snap open and thought he'd bought me a hat-box, but then I heard him stick the plug in the collar of the socket, I thought he'd bought me some sort of mixer, patent cooker or solar lamp, and then I heard a sizzling, slowly ascending rumble. Francin laid his hand gently on my shoulder and said 'Now.' And I opened my eyes, and what I saw was marvellous to behold. Francin stood there like a magician, in his fingers he held a tube, in which there shone a pale blue light, a kind of thick purple violet light, which shone on Francin's hands and face and clothes, a purple violet dampened fire in a glass tube, which Francin put close to my hand, and my arm went magnetic, I could feel purple sawdust sizzling out of that light, immaterial sparklets, which entered me and imbued me with fragrance, so that I had the scent of a summer thunderstorm, the air in the room had the scent too, like air after lightning strikes, and Francin slowly lifted the wonderful thing and put it close to his own face, I saw again that handsome profile of his, Francin stood solemnly here like Gunnar Tolnes, and then ran that tube over the open case, and there on the red plush, lining the lid as well, were set in a fan shape all kinds of brush heads, pipes and bells, all of it was made of glass and enclosed like bottles, dozens of instruments of glass, and Francin pulled off the tube and took out of the case and fixed into the bakelite holder one wonderful object after another, and each time that glass vessel glowed and filled with purple violet light, which fizzled and passed through into the human body just as required. Francin changed and experimented with all these electrodes with their neon gas content, saying quietly, 'Maryška, now Uncle Pepin can bawl his head off, now they can make trouble at the brewery, now people can insult me as they please, but here . . . here are these sparks of healing which turn into health, high frequencies which give you a new *joie de vivre*, fresh courage in life . . . Maryška, this is for you too, for your nerves, for your health, this one here is a cathode which treats your ears, this cathode here massages the heart, imagine, a heart-enhancing sizzling phosphorescence! And this one is for hysteria and epilepsy, this violet ozone removes your desire to do in public things a decent person can only think of or do at home, and other electrodes are for styes and liver-spots, torn muscles and migraine, the fifteenth one is for hyperaemia of the brain and hallucinations,' said Francin talking quietly, and in front of me spread those neon-filled forms, each one different, these electrodes were more like great pistils or stamens or orchid blooms than curative instruments. I listened to all this and for the first time ever I was speechless with surprise, even though those electrodes for

hallucinations and high frequencies for hysteria and epilepsy con-
cealed a direct reference to me, I had no reason to resist, so
benumbed was I by that purple violet beauty. Francin put on an
electrode in the form of an earpiece, he put it close to my forehead,
I looked at myself in the mirror, and there was a stunning sight! I
looked like a beautiful water maiden, like those young ladies in Art
Nouveau pictures, purple violet, with ringlets singed by the evening star! Vacuum flasks with a purple violet storm of polar radiation!
And again Francin leaned over the case and into the bakelite holder
he stuck a neon comb, this neon comb glowed like an advertising
sign over some ladies' accessories shop in Vienna or Paris, and
Francin came close to me, planted that sizzling comb in my hair, I
looked at myself in the mirror and I knew that there was nothing
more I could wish for but to comb through my tresses with that
comb. And Francin slowly, as if he knew it, ran that shining comb
through my tempestuous hair, reaching down to the ground, and
again he reared up and again he ran through it with the high fre-
quency fed comb. I began to quiver all over, I had to hug myself,
Francin breathed out quietly, every time he couldn't stop himself
from plunging his whole face into those tresses of mine, which
felt so good in that purple violet cold storm that when the comb
returned the hair ends rose with it, and again that purple violet
comb forging down through my hair, that blueish dinghy plunging
through the rapids, that cascade of my hair, that purple violet mar-
rowed hollow glass comb! 'Maryška,' Francin whispered and sat
down behind me and again slowly drew the comb through my
electric charged hair, 'Mary, this we're going to do every day now,
I brought this to assuage life's hubbub with its blue shading, qui-
eten your nerves, while for me the electrodes will rather be
coloured red, to quicken the blood circulation and invigorate the
living organism . . .' said Francin talking softly. And from the boxroom behind the kitchen hammer blows rang out, and an annoyed
and ever crosser and crosser voice rose up, Uncle Pepin, who had
come for a fortnight, and had been with us now for a whole month,
and Francin, when I stroked him under the lamp and smoothed
away his trepidation with the curve of my hand, he told me he was

horrified by the idea of Pepin staying with us twenty years, and maybe the rest of his life. And Uncle Pepin mended us our boots and shoes, in the boxroom where he also slept, but they weren't just shoes for him, they were something alive, which Uncle Pepin wrestled with, boxed to the floor, he cursed and swore for days on end, and I heard swear-words I'd never heard before, and also every half an hour Uncle took the shoe he was mending, and when he'd cursed and sworn at it, he'd slam it down, chuck it away, and then he'd sit on his stool and sulk. When he'd settled down, he would turn round slowly, take a look at the shoe, ask its forgiveness and lift it up again, stroke it, then go on pegging it and threading it tight, and having somehow clumsy fingers, he always yelped out, so that I came running, thinking he'd stuck the knife in his chest, but it was only the thread which wouldn't pull through the sole, and the whole shoe threatened to rebel, indeed did, like a wound-up spring jumping out of a gramophone, so that shoe shot away like soap out of your palm, and it leapt right up on to the cupboard or the ceiling, as if there was a little motor in it, and when it flew out of Uncle's hand, Uncle flung himself after the shoe, like a goalkeeper making a flying save of the ball . . .

And now Uncle yelled out, 'Damn! Blast!'

Francin put away the neon comb, on top of the instruments in the case he laid the sheet of plush, took a look in the direction of Uncle's cry and said:

'Those fulgurating currents have given me added strength already.' And he put the case away in the cupboard, then I pulled on the button and the window blind flew up and the china button clicked lightly against my teeth. Across the orchard I could see the beige maltings, a maltster was walking with a squat lamp in his fingers up the steps to the first floor, then he disappeared, and the lamp appeared again one storey higher, again it disappeared, and reappeared, and all the time with each stair the lamp rose as if it was walking through the dusky brewery by itself, a lamp stepping all on its own up the staircase, then the lamp disappeared, but again reappeared and walked from window to little window over the covered bridge connecting the maltings with the brewhouse.

But who was that stepping along at random like that, who was carrying that lamp about, just so that it might seem to rise up through the maltings and brewery all by itself? And I stood by the window and lurked like a hunter in wait for the buck about to come out on to the clearing . . . and my expectation made me quiver. Now the lamp appeared right up on the cooling-floor, where nobody ever goes at this hour, where there is a vat the size of an ice-hockey rink, a tank in which a whole brew of beer is put to cool, the young stuff . . . and now the lamp is walking there, a lamp that acts as if it knew I was watching it, a lamp carried just for me, the ten great big four-metre cooling-floor windows are fitted with louvres, open just a crack, like shutters in Italy and Spain, and that lamp walks steadily on, interrupted by those hundreds of louvres, the thin slivered motion of the kindled lamp, which now halts. I saw the window frame with its louvres open and someone with the lamp came out on to the roof of the ice chamber, where there is a mountain of ice piled four storeys high, twelve hundred cartloads of frozen river, of icy ceiling, which cart after cartload is heaped up in the chamber by a bucket-hoist, an ice chamber which is covered on top against the heat by half a metre of sand and river pebbles, on which from spring till autumn houseleeks grow, hundreds and thousands of houseleeks amidst cushions of green moss . . . and there stands now the squat lamp, which one of the brewery workers has brought up there, a maltster . . . I opened the window and heard from above a pleasing male voice, as if the kindled lamp were singing: '. . . the love that was, it is gone, 'twas for but a short while, golden lassie, not for long, now she is no more . . . her life is o'er . . . to the deep linn by Nymburk town she's gone . . .' And from the boxroom came Francin's shouting: 'For God's sake, give over, please, Jožko!' And slowly I went out of the room, I didn't even look today as the electric current slowly ebbed, like that love which drowned in the deep linn. Francin had lit the lamps, I went out into the passage and there sat Francin on a chair, both hands pressed to his chest and urging Uncle to leave it all be, and since he's here, couldn't he read or go to church or the pictures, just so long as there's some peace and quiet in the house . . . Francin wanted to get up, but somehow he couldn't, he tried once more, but he was intimately joined to the chair, I put my hand over my mouth, such was my alarm, because I knew that Francin had sat in the pot of cobbler's glue. Pepin was mortified, he would have liked so much to mend all of his brother's shoes, he talked about it such a lot because, of whatever he had ever felt affection for in this world, he felt affection for his brother the most, Francin tried to force his way up off the chair, but he couldn't prise himself free and he bent forward and keeled over, he lay there on the floor and the chair with him. I knelt down and tried to prise Francin free, but the cobbler's glue alias gum had stuck Francin down so firmly that he looked like an overturned statue of a seated Christ. Uncle Pepin pulled Francin's shoulders, I tried lying down behind Francin and pulling the chair in the opposite direction, but it seemed more likely that my husband and Pepin's brother would be torn in half than that we would liberate him from this situation. I rose up and something else rose with my hair, I took my hair in my fingers, drew it on to my lap and saw that my hair had got stuck in the other pot of cobbler's glue or gum, I took the scissors and snipped off the pot of glue along with the end of hair, there the little container now lay like the Golden Bull of Sicily dipped in the strings of my hair. When Francin saw what had happened to my hair, he pranced up like a horse and a lovely sound of tearing fabric ripped through the boxroom. Francin rolled over free and stood there handsome once more, his eyes filled with healthy predatory sizzling wrath, he took the lasts and pots and boxes of pegs, and Uncle Pepin, I thought the look would be enough to break his heart, but Pepin handed his brother with alacrity everything combustible, and Francin with an ever greater and growing sense of relief chucked it all in the stove. The cobbler's glue burned up so violently it lifted the stove plates, and the flame was sucked up through the flues into the chimney, a practically two-metre-long flame it was, long as my hair.

6

Uncle Pepin liked sitting best out beyond the malting floors, sheltered on one side by the orchard, on the other by the chimney stack, beside which oak staves of all sizes were stacked, staves out of which barrels were made in the cooperage, kegs, quarter hectolitres, halves and hectolitres and two hectolitres alias doubles, according to need, and then great big fifty-hectolitre and hundred-hectolitre casks, in which whole brewings of beer were stored in the fermenting rooms and cellars, casks in which the beer matured into either ordinary beer or lager. Here Uncle Pepin, when he couldn't do his cobbling, found a stick and walked up and down by the malting floors practising parade ground marches, bayonet duels. So as he wouldn't shout so much, Francin asked me to keep an eye on him.

'Am I glad to see you, sister-in-law,' said Pepin, 'your Francin's a bit of a nerves twister, a right bundle of nerves, now in Mr Batista's book he ought to give his privates a good soaking in lukewarm water or take more fresh air and exercise. But as you're here the now, we'll have a wee training session alias *Schulbildung*, seeing as I had nothing but top marks, certified commendations, no like one dunderhead, a lad from Haná, stepped out on parade and says to Colonel von Wucherer, "Mister, here's yer bullets and buns, I'm gaun home, I'm quittin' the service . . ." and the Colonel yells at the officer in charge, "Have you got the cholera or what?"'

'Peps,' I said.

'Balls!' bellowed Uncle Pepin. 'I was ever an example to all, and anyway d'ye think von Wucherer knew who I was at all? D'ye expect him to remember thousands of men like that? Once he was gaun off after the leddies, and two sodgers, dunderheads, hailed the carriage for to get a lift, then they see von Wucherer lolling back in the carriage there, and the sodgers saluted, and von Wucherer he says kindly like, "Where are you off to then, soldier lads?" And they says, "We're gaun on leave." And von Wucherer says, "Anybody gaun on leave has to have his *Urlaubsschein*, his pass, where is it?" And the sodgers felt themselves over and von Wucherer says to one of them, "What's your name, then?" and the sodger said, "Šimsa!" And von Wucherer asked the other sodger, "And what's yours?" And the other laddie said, "Řimsa!" And the sodger that said his name was Šimsa started belting off into the field, and so von Wucherer commanded, "Řimsa, bring me back that Šimsa, pronto!" Only Řimsa belted off along with Šimsa, and Colonel von Wucherer turned the carriage about and drove the stallions back to the barracks and right away he asked, "Which platoon are Šimsa and Řimsa with?" And there was no Řimsa or Šimsa in the records, so Colonel von Wucherer, that said his memory was like a photographic camera, had the whole barracks called out on parade and he went from sodger to sodger, took him by the chin and stared him close in the eye, as if he would give him a kiss any moment, for about two days, but he never recognised the one who said he was Řimsa, nor the one that called himself Šimsa, so how d'ye expect a colonel like that to remember old Peps?'

'Pssst,' said I, 'there's a meeting of the management board this afternoon.'

'Right enough,' said Uncle softly, 'but now I'm going to learn ye how many parts there are to a rifle,' and Uncle took the stick he was practising with, took it just as carefully and expertly as if it were a real army gun, pointed out on it and one by one listed off all the parts, finishing with, 'and so this is the *Kolbenschuh* or butt-end shoe, and this is the so-called *Mündung*, muzzle or mouth . . .'

'Of the Elbe,' I said.

'Balls! What are you twittering on about like a young magpie? Elbow's elbow, but this is the *Mündung*, muzzle or mouth, if you'd said the like of that to old Sergeant Brčula, he'd have socked you one and you'd have flopped over flat as a rabbit!'

From beyond the orchard you could hear the irate slamming of windows in the office and Francin ran out of the counting-house in a white shirt. I could see him dashing through the long grass, dodging the branches of the trees, it was a lovely sight to see the man running along, jumping over obstructions with leg outstretched to keep his footing in the grass, the other above the grass in an almost horizontal posture, his legs repeating alternately all of that wonderful top-of-the-grass-hopping motion. When he reached us I saw that in his fingers he was clutching a number three lettering pen.

'You pair of uhlans, what are you getting up to again?'

'We're playing at being soldiers,' I said.

'Play whatever you like, but be quiet about it, the girl in accounts has just spilt a whole bottle of ink!' Francin shouted softly.

'Where are we supposed to play then?' says I.

'Wherever you like, climb up the chimney if you want, just as long as we can't hear you . . . she's spattered a whole journal with ink!' cried Francin. The sleeves of his white shirt were tucked up at the elbows with elastic bands, he turned about, no longer running now, he waded through the tall grass, I looked after him, and he turned back, I kissed my hand and blew that kiss like a downy feather after him.

'The chimney?' said Pepin with surprise.

'The chimney,' I said.

And Francin disappeared behind the branches, his white shirt now went into the office.

'So then: Direktion!' exclaimed Uncle Pepin, mounting the first cramp-iron, and then, thinking better of it, he jumped down and said, 'After you.'

And that which I had dreamed of since my very first day at the brewery, finding the strength to climb up the brewery chimney stack, there it was protruding and rising up before me. I leaned my head back and took hold of the first cramp-iron, the perspective ran back upwards in ever diminishing and diminishing rungs, that sixty-metre chimney from that foreshortened angle resembled an aimed heavy gun, I was allured by the fluttering green leotard which someone had tied to the lightning conductor, and that green leotard, while there was a breeze below, that green leotard fluttered and right through the open window I could hear that green leotard making the din of rattling tin, and I caught hold of the first rung, freed a hand and untied the green bow that bound my hair together, and quickly I went up hand over hand, my legs like coupled axles took on the same rhythm. Halfway up the chimney I felt the first buffet of streaming air, my hair was buoyed up, almost ran ahead of me, suddenly all of me was centred in my loose trailing hair, which spread out and enveloped me like music, several times my hair landed on a rung, I had to watch out and slow down the work of my legs, because I was stepping on my own hair, ah, now if Bod'a had been here, he would have held up my hair for me, he would have been changed to an angel, and in his flight he would have kept watch to see that my hair didn't get caught in the spokes and chain, this chimney climbing of mine was a bit like my bicycle riding. I waited a moment, the wind seemed to have taken it into its head to get a taste of my hair, it lifted and ruffled it so that I had the feeling I was hanging by my hair on a knot tied several rungs above me, then the wind suddenly lulled, my hair untied itself and slowly, like the loosened golden hands on the church tower clock, my hair was falling, as if out of my head a golden peacock spread open wide and then slowly closed its tail. And I used this lull and quickly went up hand over hand, coordinating the motion of my legs with the work of my arms, until I laid my whole hand on the chimney rim, for a moment I recovered my breath like a swimming competitor at the end of a race in the pool, and then I pulled myself up with both arms as if out of the water, cast a leg over the rim, caught hold of the lightning conductor and slowly, as if out of syrup, drew up my other leg. I gathered my hair behind me, sat myself down and tossed my hair over my lap. And suddenly a wind rose and my hair slipped out of my hand, and my golden tresses fluttered out just like last year before the first spring day, my hair flamed out like tendrils of weed in a shallow swift stream, I held on to the lightning conductor with one hand and felt as if I was the goddess of the hunt Diana with a lance, my cheeks burned with rapture and I felt that if I did nothing else in this little town but climb up to the top of this chimney, that might not be much, but I could live on the strength of that for numbers of years, maybe even a whole lifetime. And I leaned forward and from the depth I saw how tiny Uncle Pepin was, just a little wee angel with a head and arms, I wondered how up till now I had the impression that Uncle Pepin's hair was thick and curly, but now I saw his bald head rising towards me with its sparse circlet of hair, now that head laid itself on the very rim, out from under it pulled another palm and caught hold of the edge, he looked at me and his face likewise beamed with happiness. He pulled himself up on to the chimney, and as if unconsciously propped one arm at his waist and shaded with the other his eyes.

'Good God, sister-in-law,' he said with amazement, 'this would make a brilliant *Beobachtungsstelle* or observation post.'

'Alias viewing tower,' I appended.

'Bollocks! A viewing tower's for civilians, but an observation post alias *Beobachtungsstelle*'s for the military, for the military in time of war to follow the movements of the enemy! Sister-in-law, and you such an intellectual beauty too, if Captain Tonser heard you say that, he'd sock you with his sabre, yelling out, "I'll have your frigging nuts for mincemeat!"'

'Peps,' said I, splashing my legs in the wellspring of air.

'For Christ's sake, what would he be having my nuts for mincemeat for? He liked me, I used to carry his sabre!' choked Uncle Pepin, leaning over me, and his face was ominous and threatening like a stone gargoyle on the church roof.

'Och, never mind!' I gave a wave of the hand. 'Isn't it beautiful up here, Uncle Jožin?'

And I looked over the low-lying landscape, edged with hills and woodlands, I looked at the town and saw how you can only get into our little town by crossing water, how it's really an island town, above the town the river which flowed around the town divided in two and past the walls two watercourses flowed, which joined up again beyond the town in one river, I saw how actually each road leading through the town and out has two bridges, two crossings, while across the river there is a white stone-built bridge, on which people were standing, leaning on the side-wall and looking over to the brewery chimney, looking at me and Uncle Pepin, at my hair flapping in the breeze, and in the sunlight that hair of mine glittered and shone like a papal banner, while down below the air was calm and still. Across the river there towered the big church, and at the height of my face was the golden clock-face on the tower, and round the church in concentric circles stretched the streets and lanes and houses and buildings. Festooned from every window like feather quilts, petunias and carnations and red pelargoniums projected themselves, the whole of this small town was edged with a lacework of walls and from above it resembled a cut chalcedony. And on to that white bridge the fire tender hurtled with its hose, the firemen's helmets glittered and the bugler held his golden trumpet and bugled 'Fire!' and all the firemen wore white hessian uniforms, the red tender thundered across the bridge like an orchestrion, the firemen held on to the rungs standing upright on that clattering fire-engine altar that now dipped behind the buildings and gardens.

'Is it true, Uncle Jožin, you used to graze goats right up at the front line?' I said.

'Whoever told you that?' bellowed Uncle Pepin and sat down on the rim, then lay down on his back, folding his arms behind his head.

'Melichar, the tobacconist,' I said.

'What would a tobacconist and invalid to boot be doing in the war?' roared Uncle.

'Melichar was a captain apparently in the war, yesterday Captain Melichar said, "God forbid it should come to war and I should have that Pepin chap drilling under me,"' said I, holding on to the lightning conductor and looking down at the brewery. And again I wondered to see how the brewery was right outside the town, how it was surrounded all round by a wall, with the little town on the other side, but how along the walls there are tall trees of maple and ash, which also form a square shape, and how this brewery resembled a monastery or a kind of fortress, or prison, how every wall was topped not only with barbed wire, but each and every wall and pillar had set in concrete on its topmost bricks jagged fragments of green bottles, which glittered from above like amethysts and amaranths.

'How would he have seen me anyway . . . even if I did graze those goats?' said Uncle, and went on lying there gazing up at the sky, one leg hooked over his bent knee and swinging the free ankle.

'With a telescope,' said I.

'But would the Emperor lend a telescope to any old tobacconist?' said Uncle.

'As a captain Melichar was issued with two telescopes,' I said, and saw how on the bridge there were now as many people as swallows about to migrate and someone was peering at me from the bridge through a telescope. I gave a smile into that telescope and out of the depths a wind arose and my hair started to splay out like a fan of ostrich plumes, I saw how around my eyes streams of hair were closing in upwards, round the whole of my sitting figure there was a kind of Halo like the one on the plague column for the Virgin Mary, Our Lady of the Seven Sorrows, on the column in the town square . . .

'And if it came to war, what would happen if Melichar was to have me under him, eh?' enquired Pepin and it seemed to me he was grappling with ever growing torpor.

'He said, if war came again, he'd just crook his little finger on drill like so . . . and call out, *"Pepin zu mir!"* And you'd come rushing over with your tongue hanging out and paying your respects and go down before him on one knee,' said I, and when I took a look, Uncle Pepin was asleep, he'd fallen sound asleep, he was lying on the rim of the chimney, which had a slight sway in it, I only noticed it now from that recumbent statue of Uncle Pepin, how we were both perceptibly swaying, as if we were sitting on some kind of pendulum hung in the sky. And the firemen sped from the cross, the horses looked from above as if they had bolted, their back legs were strung out in the harness and their fore legs were shooting straight out in front of their heads, like snails sticking out their horns, the whole of that fire-fighting contraption glittered like a child's plaything and threatened any minute to fall apart and the pieces of the vehicles would go scattering just like that military vehicle in Truhlářská Street when the grenades it was carrying exploded. And there at the chief's post stood the chief of the firemen, Mr de Giorgi, member of the management board of the brewery on whose chimney I was seated, a chimney sweep who was also the fire-chief, for instead of just a flat to live in he had a fire-fighting museum, everything that had ever burned down Mr de Giorgi had photographed, he even got hold of photographs from before the blaze, and so on all the walls of his flat he had photographs, always in pairs, a cow before the fire and after it, a dog before the fire and after, an adult male before the fire and after, a barn before the fire and after it, all things, all animals, all persons burnt or affected by fire, all these Mr de Giorgi would photograph, and now to be sure he was only riding off to the brewery because, if it collapsed, he would have a photograph of the brewery manager's wife before the collapse and one after the collapse . . . and now this fire-fighting orchestrion entered the bend in the road at the brewery gate, the wheels grated and the fire-engine disappeared behind the office, and I was just thinking the firemen must have overturned along with the horses, when they rode out again nobly and trumpeting and then the fire-engine drove right up under the chimney . . . I thought they'd probably start to use their hose in a minute, they'd shower the water right up as high as the top of the chimney, Mr de Giorgi would request me to step out on to the very summit of that gushing geyser, and then slowly they'd start to turn down the tap and I would descend from above on the declining peak of the water spout, but the firemen dashed out of the engine, knelt down, saluted each other with axes and suddenly spread out a big sheet, six firemen stretched out that sheet, they leaned back and gazed upwards, but the sway of the chimney stack was evidently such that the firemen with the sheet had to shift this way and that according to the probable likelihoods of my fall.

And the members of the management board came riding along in their traps, before they came at a trot, but today those traps came rattling along the roads, from the villages and the town, the horses peltering along at a canter and a gallop. And all those traps not as before, when they stopped outside the office, this time all of them gathered in the brewery yard, where the coopers and the bottlers and the maltsters and everybody stood and all of them gazing upwards with their heads thrown back, as if expecting from on high Jesus' return or the descending of the Holy Spirit upon them. And now the chairman of the brewery, Doctor Gruntorád in person, rode in from the cross, feudal scion and admirer of the old Austria, as always he sat there on the box holding the reins in his deerskin riding gloves, his inimitable hat elegantly poised over his eyes, smoking his cigarette and biting into its amber holder, and driving the black stallion on into the brewery, while his coachman with a rueful smile lolled back on the plush seat like a lord . . .

And down below Mr de Giorgi issued vain instructions to the firemen to climb the chimney, finally Mr de Giorgi determined to climb the chimney himself. And his white uniform ascended, pausing often, but continuing again to climb up the rungs, until his helmet finally emerged at my feet.

'Uncle Jožin,' I shook Uncle who was lying at my feet and Uncle sat up, rubbed his eyes, and leapt up in shock clutching the lightning conductor. Mr de Giorgi hopped up on to the rim, regained his breath, removed his helmet and mopped the sweat with his handkerchief.

'In the name of the law,' he said, 'missus, please climb down. And your brother-in-law too.'

'Mr de Giorgi, don't you feel giddy?' says I.

'I say, in the name of the law, climb down,' repeated Mr de Giorgi.

'And I say, Mr de Giorgi first?' says I.

'No,' said Mr de Giorgi gazing into the bowels of the chimney, 'for training reasons I shall descend by the inside of the stack,' he appended.

I held on to the lightning conductor, put my foot on the rung, turned about and my hair blazed up, again that draught from the depth inflated my tresses, they fanned out for the last time, as if they knew it, one last time that golden mane of mine flamed above the brewery chimney, again I blessed with my hair like a huge golden monstrance all those who looked upon me at that moment, and Mr de Giorgi himself was affected by what he saw.

'We are witnesses to an extraordinary incident, missus, what a pity ladies can't serve as firemen,' he said and picked up his trumpet, a tiny little trumpet which resembled a ticket conductor's clippers, he blew on it, but that blowing was so melancholic, like a trussed kid bleating in the slaughterhouse trap, then he kissed my hand and I descended, quickly I hurried down, so as to keep ahead of my hair, which I threatened to tread on, getting embroiled and sending myself plummeting to the depths. And suddenly I saw around me the tops of trees, then I seemed to descend into the branches and from out of the branches I finally laid my foot on terra firma.

'That was just beautiful,' said Doctor Gruntorád with delight, 'but you deserve twenty-five of the best . . .'

'On the bare bottom,' I said.

'What were you doing there, for goodness' sake?' enquired the doctor.

'Well, as you said, it was just beautiful, and as it was beautiful, so it was dangerous, and as it was dangerous, so it was just absolutely truly made for me . . .' I said, and Francin stood there pallid, his head on his chest, in his frock coat, white cuffs and gutta-percha collar and his tie in the shape of a cabbage leaf.

And the mechanics opened the great doors of the chimney, soot came tumbling out, and that black glittering cavern was as large as a summerhouse. Uncle Pepin leapt off the last rung and said:

'So the Austrian Soldat wins another glorious victory, eh?'

But all were staring into the black chamber at the base of the chimney.

'What regiment were you? Who were you under?' Doctor Gruntorád enquired.

'Freiherr von Wucherer,' Uncle Pepin gave a salute.

'*Ruht*,' barked the doctor, and added, 'Manager, what is your brother able to do?'

'He qualified as a shoemaker and worked three years in a brewery,' answered Francin.

'Well then, Manager, take your brother and put him up in the maltings quarters. The best cure for loudmouths is work,' said Doctor Gruntorád.

And in the black cavern a white trouser leg emerged, almost right up at the ceiling of this bower overgrown with soot, the leg groped for the rung, but evidently there wasn't one, so the leg gyrated away there as if Mr de Giorgi was pedalling a bicycle. And the deputy chief of the firemen issued a command and the firemen ran with their rescue sheet into the chimney, spread the sheet out, and the deputy chief called up into the sooty grime, 'Chief, let go! We're here! We've brought the rescue sheet!'

And Mr de Giorgi let go of the rungs, first of all soot and coal-dust poured out of the chimney, poured out in front of the chimney, tender soft curly little molehills of soot, then coughing resounded and the firemen ran out totally blackened, bearing something in their rescue sheet, as if they had landed some huge pike fish or wels, and they laid the sheet on the ground and out of the soot and dust popped up the totally black figure of Mr de Giorgi, laughing, with white creases of laughter wrinkling all the way across his black visage. Mr de Giorgi drew out his trumpet, blew on it, and declared, 'And so we may deem the rescue work accomplished.'

And he came forward out of the heap of soot and stretched out both arms and extracted congratulations and walked about the place all self-assured and joyfully stiff and wooden and I saw that Mr de Giorgi would live off the memory of that descent by the inside of the chimney not just a couple of years, but all the remainder of his days.

7

At the corner of the maltings there was always such a draught, such a wind, that I had to walk practically leaning forward, or turn round and lie back into the gust as into a rocking chair. That gusting sucked up my hair like a hungry smoker sucking on a cigarette. But no sooner had I pushed through this stumbling-block of air, by the door to the maltings there was such a breathless calm, that I fell straight over on my knees or back. And yet I always looked forward with pleasure to this air combat, in which I had to fight for possession of my towels. Once the wind snatched away a bouclé bath wrap, all I could do was grab at it with my hand, and the draught, having its sense of humour, flicked it away from me, I reached out again when the bath towel was very nearly about to touch my hair, but the gust hopped away nimbly a bit further with that great towel wrap, and when it floated down again, I leapt after it, but the gust carried it away up with drawn-out laughter, like a kite that bouclé towel bobbed up in the autumn sky, a white zig-zag-dancing wrap moving to the rhythm of the wind, and it vanished in the darkness over the maltings. And yet it was beautiful, to let yourself be handled on the lips of the breeze, to let yourself fill with the aroma of that windy bath like a peppermint sweet. Then when I felt the doorhandle, the draught from the other side of the door leaned bodily against the door so that I too had to press bodily on that door, but the draught, which had its sense of humour, suddenly stopped and I fell into the dark passage on to my knee. Once I staggered and crashed into a maltster, who fell, but in his fall still kept holding the burning lamp so neatly that it didn't break. Then, with palm outstretched as though to ward off a storm, I felt the handle to the engine room, the smell of oil and hemp engulfed me warmly like a bath, I closed the door, felt for the key and locked it. Then I lit a candle. The huge distribution wheel sketched out a silvery arc in the spindrift half-darkness, the taut distribution cables gleamed and glittered with oil. The dynamos and motors were like fat African beasts, the oil cans like birds pecking insects off those hippos. Slowly I undressed, turning on the taps of hot water, which ran from a huge boiler into a hundred-hectolitre barrel cut in half. I took off my clothes and listened to the draught whistling through the floors of the maltings right up to the drying-room and rattling the shutters there. And I got into that great big wooden bath, the water is always so hot that I have to turn on the cold water taps, I sit there squatting and the hotness of the water hurts me till my teeth chatter, until the cold water mixes in with the boiling hot, then slowly I settle down and lie back, stretching myself right out. I lie there in that barrel cut in half like the needle in a compass box, I gaze up above myself to the beams where the white boiler vanishes, and I dream, I start to dream, I slowly dissolve in the hot water, like soap powder I float in the hot water, all my limbs relax, I untie all the cloths and sheets into which my past life is wrapped and bound, I open all the baskets and cases and cupboards in which there are images which happened long ago, but which are ever willing to visit me again, beautiful, but colourless images which only in the bath acquire their finishing touches and precise colourings. These are my moving pictures, projected on the screen of my closed eyes, the film whose script and direction were shot by my own life, the film in which I play the lead role, I, who have come now to this spot, this wooden bath, in which I lie . . . I am a little lassie with straw plaits, I play chuckie stones in the middle of the road, I sit cross-legged and scatter the four stones again, ready to take one and throw it up and gather up the three remaining ones in time to catch the first as it falls. Approaching thunder, I fall on my back the moment after scattering the four pebbles, the sky darkens and above me loom terrible maws and buckles and reins, hooves flash over me with their glittering shoes, I close my eyes, dried mud spatters over me, the thundering moves away onward, I get to my feet and see the clattering vehicle drawn by bolting horses, I see the blue sky and out of it leaning over me the head of my worried dad. I am a little lassie, playing on the field track with chuckie stones, my dad always took me off behind the building for safety's sake, so nothing would happen to me. I see two soldiers running from the woods, I see them running along the meadow path where I am playing, these soldiers are running like two bolting horses, I lie down on my back so as not to be run over, I see the soldiers leaping up, I see above me the soles of the boots full of studs, then the shadow of the soldiers thundered across me and the thump of the army boots dinned and departed down the meadow track. I sat up and saw the soldiers running to the stream – they stop, instead of a footbridge there is a beam hung on chains, the soldiers splay their arms like the two guardian angels over my bed their wings, and then they run over to the other side and run on, in the curve of the track I see their rising shining studs for the last time, now they vanish in the forest bend. The soldiers vanished long ago, but I am still thinking of them. I see myself now, I toddle down to the stream, I put my little shoe on the log, I see the water swirling in the stream, I splay my arms and run along the log, but right in the middle the log slips from under me and I fall into the water – I pedalled away in the depths like Mum on her sewing machine, but I couldn't get a footing on the bottom, at first I drank water, but then I had probably drunk enough water to make me drown, all I saw was how my hair fell free and fluttered along the bottom of the stream and mingled with the green tendrils of weed and water flowers without blooms, I wanted so awfully much to sleep, I couldn't close my eyes, and everything was full of light and I seemed to be seeing the sky above me through thick spectacles . . . and then I awaken, I see how beautiful it is to be drowned, as if I were at home, lying in heaven in a little bed just like the one we had at home – I saw my hands resting on the feather quilt with forget-me-nots printed over it just like the one that Mummy has, and opposite me hangs a picture of a guardian angel, just like the one we have, and then Mummy came in and said, 'Just come on in, children, come along in . . .' and into the kitchen came the little girls from the neighbourhood, and now I knew I was drowned, because the girls, who called me Mary and I called them Hedvig and Evie and Boženka, those girls put holy pictures next to my hands on the quilt, all over my bed there were so many little pictures of guardian angels, and Hedvig said to me, 'Mummy told me you were drowned . . .' and she put down another holy picture, and I said, 'Why are you giving me that picture then?' And Hedvig said, 'You put them in little dead girls' coffins . . .' and I was crying, because that meant I was really quite quite dead, but then my mummy came in, bringing candies, and when she saw so many little holy pictures Mummy said, 'But girls, Mary's not dead, Doctor Michálek poured all the water out of her and breathed new life into her with his breath . . .' and the little girls were disappointed and sorry that there wasn't going to be a funeral, that I hadn't died, because they already saw themselves in their white dresses made of curtains and burning in their fingers a big candle decorated with myrtle, and the brass band would play such melancholy music and the girls would go in the procession and they would have their hair all in little curls and they would be crying because I had drowned . . . but now it's off, this procession, and the crying, all because of those two women who went out to soak their laundry and pulled me out and took me home . . . Dad was so infuriated that time, ah, my dad could be angry like nobody else, Mum bought four wardrobes a year, old cupboards from the secondhand dealer, and whenever Dad got really cross, Mum took him off quick to the summer-house and put an axe in his hand and first Dad would break up the back walls, and then he would smash and curse at the rest of the wardrobe, ripping out the door with such zest and then demolishing the whole cupboard from the side like a matchbox, and after half an hour, when he'd chopped up the wardrobe into splinters, Mum always had such a lot of firewood for kindling and heating . . . and I heard Dad shouting and carrying on about how I'd drowned myself, how I still couldn't behave like a decent little girl should, because the other girls don't do such things, I got such a fright that I slipped out of the quilt, put my clothes on and ran out into the yard, and there stood a goods lorry, I clambered up on the back, there by the rear window stood a barrel, I sneaked into that barrel, and it was warm in there, I fell asleep, and when I awoke, I could hear the goods lorry going along, and when I got up I could see through the window that it was getting dark, that close by the rear window was a man's cap, when I looked from the side I could see it was Mr Brabec, and I stuck my hand through and scratched Mr Brabec behind the ear and said, 'Mr Brabec, I'm in here . . .' and Mr Brabec let go the steering wheel and yelled out, and the lorry stopped so sharply that the barrel rolled over in which I was crouched up to the shoulders, and I tumbled out on to the floor and off the floor on to the ground, and I picked myself up from the road and dusted off my wee skirt, and Mr Brabec ran this way and yelled and stamped, and I said, 'Mr Brabec, really, it's me it is.' But Mr Brabec moaned and keeled over, and when the officers came, they put a blanket over Mr Brabec, but that wasn't enough, one of the officers had to strip almost naked and lie on top of Mr Brabec to keep him warm, later at the police station one of the officers told me I could have been the death of the man, and I remembered Dad and how he would have to smash up another wardrobe, and the officer laid me a fur-coat on the floor and then he took a rope and tied me by the leg to the table leg, and there I lay and wept, above me rocked the soles of boots full of studs, one leg crossed over the other, and I was tied there by the leg to the table leg, and then I fell asleep and Dad appeared over me, kneeling and resting on both arms like legs, they untied me from the table, and when they pulled me out by the arm the officers were so accusing that Dad took the rope and tied that rope round my neck and I burst into tears and called out, 'Daddy, I don't want you to hang me. I don't want to die on the branch so long . . .' you see, once the cat ate Dad's liver and Dad hung the cat on a branch for doing that, and the cat he didn't die till the next day . . . and Dad led me off on the end of the rope to the train, and when we arrived home, Dad led me like a calf on the end of the rope, explaining to everyone how I wasn't a decent little girl and how he had to lead me on the end of a rope like a bad dog . . . and at home Dad, as soon as Mum saw Dad, straightaway she handed him the axe, I expected Dad to chop off my head just like he did to the turkey cocks and hens, but Dad hurled himself straight at the wardrobe and with one blow smashed through the back wall and with one more swipe of the body, sideways, he smashed through the rest of the cupboard, so that it all fell flat on the ground, like trampling a carton . . . All soap-suddy, I lie there covered in foam, lathering myself and not even noticing, thinking and remembering the images lying deep in the depths of time, images constantly returning, clarifying, augmenting one another. I am a six-year-old girl with loose flowing hair, on the crown of my head it is just caught with little blue ribbon bows, Dad hasn't broken a single wardrobe on my behalf for a whole year, it's Sunday noon and I am walking through the little square, in the open windows curtains flutter, you hear the chinking of cutlery and plates, the draught draws out the savour of food, yesterday Dad bought me a sailor suit and umbrella, I stand in front of the water fountain, then I lean over and look at my mirrored hair, coins gleam on the bottom, we think if you throw some money into the water fountain you may have a wish come true, for safety's sake I threw two twenty-heller bits into the fountain and wished that I should never drown again, never run away from home, and always be a decent little girl, especially when Daddy bought me such lovely clothes and an umbrella. I hopped up on the edge of the fountain to see better how nice I looked in that sailor's jacket, I looked about, no one was coming, no one was looking out of the window to complain to Daddy, I hopped up on the fountain, and when I leaned over, I saw the lovely pleated skirt and little white sockies and shiny polished shoes, I shook out my hair, and when I looked again at myself reflected in the water, I overbalanced and fell into the fountain, and the water swallowed me up like a great fish when it swallows a tiny little one, again I tried to find the bottom with my shiny little shoe, but the bottom of the fountain was deeper than I was tall, and again I surfaced for air, but I was too frightened to call for help, because Daddy would be too cross, and I was on my way to join the angels, again I was enveloped in a bright sweet world, as if I were a bee fallen into honey. I saw how my head fell slowly to the bottom, beside my eye I saw that twenty-heller coin which I had thrown into the fountain with the wish that I should never drown again, my skirt welled up so grandly and my hair washed across my face and again so slowly the hair grandly returned, and then I wanted to sleep and only moved my legs about very slowly, much more slowly than Mummy pedalling on her sewing machine, and for the last time I saw the little bubbles rising from my mouth, as if I was a bottle of soda or mineral water . . . but again I didn't drown, one lady saw me, Mrs Krsenská, who had been ten years in a wheelchair and had stomach ulcers, she had been looking out of her window just at the moment I fell in, and one gentleman came running over, Mr Pokorný the photographer, who jumped in after me still with his knife and fork and napkin tucked under his chin, and pulled me out. I woke up on the steps of the fountain, I had the impression it was raining, I took my little umbrella and spread it open, but actually the midday sun was shining and the bell finishing striking the midday hour, Mr Pokorný was leaning over me, water dropped from his napkin and a couple of frizzles of cabbage with it, Mr Pokorný was threatening me with the knife and fork in turn, saying if his dinner had got cold he was going to see to me again, because nice little girls if they want to drown themselves, do it at a proper time and not on the dot of twelve, when the first of the goose is on the table, and I looked and there in all the windows stood the townspeople in their shirts and waistcoats and all holding a fork in one hand and a knife in the other and all of them were looking down at me with annoyed expressions on their faces and indicating that what they'd really like to do was stick me on their forks and cut me up with their knives, and so I stood up and so much water gushed out of me that I thought the clouds had burst, I bowed, not that I wanted to make fun of them, but meaning that I recognized the point and knew I shouldn't have done it just when the first of the geese were on the roasting pans on a Sunday at noon . . . Now I lie in the brewery bath, in that hundred-hectolitre barrel cut in half, someone walks from the malting floor up to the lodgings where Uncle Pepin now lives too, and out of that hall resounds his frightful roar, 'Doh re mi fa so la ti doh . . .' and then again the descending scale, 'Doh ti la so fa mi re doh,' just as the water runs out with the dregs of soap deposit. Someone climbs from the malting floor up to the lodgings, probably it's the young maltster, sweat-soaked and with a ring under one eye, as if he'd fallen on top of a telescope, a ring neatly stamped like a round postmark, it's bound to be him, now he climbs slowly with his shirt tossed over his shoulder and in one hand he's carrying the squat lamp like an emperor his imperial orb, and in the other hand the turning shovel like an imperial sceptre, so he climbs upwards, pauses on the landing and sings that sweet song . . . 'the love that was, it is gone, 'twas for but a short while, golden lassie, not for long, now she is no more . . . her life is o'er . . . to the deep linn by Nymburk town she's gone . . .' Quickly I got dressed, tied my hair up in a towel, blew out the candle with a mighty puff and went out into the dark, with my palm stretched out before me, till a dim light trickled out at the bend in the passage from the depths of the malting floor, with yellow lines it edged the angles of the damp steps. From the malting floor resounded the melodic tender tapping of the turning shovels on the wet floor, the rhythmic hiss of the shovelled barley . . . and again that song like a rising sea-tide . . . 'the love that was, it is gone . . .' for a moment I stood in the half-darkness, then I descended a couple of steps, the warmth of the germinated barley slapped me on the cheeks, two tubby lamps lit up the beds of barley, paraffin lamps on wooden tripods in the middle of fields of barley, the young maltster stripped to the waist was skipping along with short little paces, gathering shovelfuls of barley from one side and tossing that malt on to the other side and leaving a furrow behind him, as if that labouring wooden shovel were the keel of a boat that cleaves the waves in front but leaves behind smoothness closing in, that handsome maltster lad with every step turned over a shovelful of golden barley and with every shovel his back gleamed more and more with sweat . . . 'the love that was, it is gone . . .' the male voice went on filling the low vault of the malting floor, a vault resting on four avenues of black iron pillars . . . now the young lad stood erect like King Barleycorn, the ring beneath his eye sparkled like a spectacle rim, his trunk was altogether swathed in the shining quicksilver of sweat . . . and I went on hearing that song, someone else was singing that elegy now, someone working several fields of barley away, where that second tubby paraffin lamp stood on its wooden tripod . . . the young maltster wiped his face with the full of his palm and discarded a whole handful of sweat . . . I walked on further, my legs were wobbling under me, there a little wee man was turning the barley, he looked more like a pensioned-off jockey, in overalls and beret, he'd just finished one heap, now he took the shovel, scooped up the barley at the edge, and then again those swift little maltster's paces, the man was almost running, he ruffled the scooped-up barley and the shovel left an exactly cut border in its wake. When this little wee maltster finished off this job and bent and placed in the corner his crossed shovels as his trademark, he straightened up and sang beautifully . . . ''twas for but a short while, golden girlie, not for long, now she is no more . . . her life is o'er . . .' This was Mr Jirout, the little maltster, who when he met me greeted me always guiltily and with a constant smile, Francin used to tell of him that in his younger days Mr Jirout had been an artiste, shot out of a cannon at fairs, to the rolling of drums they tied him up live in a little blue satin suit, put him into the wooden gun-carriage, then the impresario applied the bluely smouldering fuse, and when the deafening bang came, flame spouted from the mouth of the cannon and then Mr Jirout in person, arms tensed, who upon reaching the apex of his trajectory, spread his arms out wide and fell into the waiting trampoline, scattering smiles and coloured paper roses and blown kisses. When he landed, he jumped up, bounced on the trampoline and bowed and received his ovation, at every fair and every country wake. Once they packed little Mr Jirout into his cannon, and when they shot him out and Mr Jirout reached the apex of his trajectory, he spread his arms out wide and as he fell head foremost slowly downwards he saw he had already gone far beyond the trampoline, the impact in the gun-carriage was stronger than it had ever been before, but all the same Mr Jirout went on smiling and scattering his smiles and coloured paper roses and blown kisses, only to smash himself up beyond the fencing in a pile of timber. After they'd spent a year putting Mr Jirout back on his feet, he found he'd lost the desire to go on scattering his blown kisses and roses, he withdrew from the life of an artiste like a banknote no longer in circulation, and for the last eight years, after getting fully back in the pink, he's been working in the brewery as a maltster . . . 'the love that was, it is gone, 'twas for but a short while . . .'

8

Uncle Pepin had been working in the brewery for three weeks now; the coopers took him on, and from then on there was merriment in the brewery. When I had a chance, I took some buckets for draff and went across the brewery yard, the foreman looked at me searchingly to see if he should bring a two-litre pot of beer, I nodded, and while I collected the draff from the wagon, the coopers were having their morning break, Uncle Pepin was lying on his back and on his chest an empty cask of keg, the cooper men were laughing fit to burst, choking on crumbs of spread slices of bread, and Uncle Pepin sang, 'Doh re mi fa so la ti doh!'

The assistant cooper knelt over Uncle, saying, 'Now, Mr Josef, let's have that scale backwards, just like Caruso and Mařáček used to practise it!'

And Uncle Pepin cleared his throat and screeched horrifically, 'Doh ti la so fa mi re doh . . .'

And when the workmen had had their fill of this din, the assistant cooper said, 'And now, Mr Josef, give us a high C.'

And the cooper men stood up, leaned over Uncle Pepin, who screeched out that high C, and the cooper men roared with laughter, lay on their backs with their spread slices of bread, and hopped up again and choked over their crumbs and rested against the cooperage and chuckled and chuckled, to avoid asphyxiating with mirth.

And in the middle of the yard the old maltster Mr Řepa roasted the malt for the dark ale, he sat on a chair and turned the black drum on its shaft, and under that drum the charcoal burned bluely and pinkly and redly, and the old maltster, with his scattering of grey hairs, majestically and regularly revolved the soot-caked globe like some god from an ancient myth of earthly spheres.

And the assistant cooper leaned over Uncle and said, 'And now once again, one last breath exercise, sing us another high C, and this time sing it in the head . . . but watch you don't do a job in your pants, or give yourself brown trousers!'

And Uncle Pepin breathed in, screwed up his nose, and the cooper men leaned over him and Uncle sang inside of himself that high C, the kind of long drawn-out note made by a creaking gate, he sang that high C with all his might and main, he kept that inward singing note going a whole minute, and then he was so exhausted, he spread his arms and breathed out and the cask on his chest heaved, just like in the music academies when the pupils lie on their backs on the carpet and the teacher piles books on their chests.

And I stepped along with my pails of draff past the open door to the boiler house, there in the half-dark glowed the lower hemisphere of the boiler, the ash-box shining with the saffron shade of the burning coal on the grate, down through the glowing ash-box tumbled red and purple violet burning coals and green-blue cinders, and right next to it in the darkness glowed the open boiler with its beige tinge, and there the workman crouched like a child in the mother's womb tapping the scale out of the boiler in that cramped position, two light bulbs lit up sharply that workman crouched there in an arc, as he worked in the dust and sang with it, encircled by cables of the electric circuit like an umbilical cord. Each time I glimpsed out of the sunlight that sharply lit oval and that workman tapping away bit by bit with a hammer, I thought that anyone going past would be startled by this image framed in the lunette, but no one even paused for thought, no one was sorry, nor was he sorry for himself either, that man who spent a fortnight on end like a woodpecker tapping saltpetre in his crouched position, on the contrary, he sang with it.

And the coopers had finished their break, the foreman cooper stood like a shepherd among sheep, around him hundred of barrels, he leaned over one of them, examined it with a searching eye, then he straightened and pulled up a burning candle on a twisted wire from the wame of the barrel, and again he leant over another barrel and dangled the candle into its interior scanning it with a watchful eye to see whether the barrel was fit to be filled with beer or whether it had to be caulked, that is to say pitched. Uncle Pepin stood by the enormous stove and stoked it with anthracite and coke, heated up the pitch, the stove thundered darkly away and out of its short bent chimney there erupted a red fire hemmed with blue borders, flames ornamented with a sizzling green corona, like the flame on a blow-lamp used to thaw out frozen joints or burn off old paint.

The carters loaded the wet barrels of beer into the carts, and carried out casks of ice. The foreman handed me a measure of orange-coloured beer, a measure full of drops of condensed steam. And I knew the foreman didn't like me, and that he would have given me not one, but five measures of beer, and more, as long as I would drink them, drink them down, and the workmen would see what an inclination to drunkenness the manager's wife possessed. But I was young, and hence above all that, whatever I did, I did, only asking prior permission of myself, and always I nodded my own assent, and that inward nodding of mine, that sign from my mentor, who was somewhere in my heart inside, that consent went straight to my blood, and my hand stretched out and I sipped with gusto, with such gusto, that the carters stopped stacking the barrels and stared at me. So I stood by the ramp, alongside the horses, Ede and Kare seemed to have an understanding with me, their manes and great tails had that same colour of golden beer. And old Řepa in the middle of the brewery yard now pulled out the crank-shaft, examined expertly the contents of roasted malt and nodded to himself, pulled a handle and swung that black globe on the mechanism away from the red-hot coals, loosened the lock carefully with a small hammer, turned the handle, and the hot roasted malt tumbled out on to the black griddle and the aroma of malt shot off on all sides. It must have reached the square by now, and the passers-by will be turning their heads towards the brewery, where in the middle the old maltster mumbles contentedly and rakes through the roasted malt with a black wooden poker.

And Uncle Pepin stood by the pitching stove and smiled at me, he wore a leather apron, the furnace behind him thundered and threatened red-hot to explode into the air like some kind of fantastic rocket from a Jules Verne novel. That flame which sizzled out after Uncle Pepin was so terrifically beautiful, that I took a look about me, but no one was marvelling at the display. And the master cooper came and began passing the barrels down the skid to Uncle Pepin's feet, and Uncle Pepin took every barrel, heaved it on to his knee and stuck it on the pin of the nozzle, pressed the foot lever, and boiling pitch squirted into the barrel, and Uncle Pepin lifted the barrel and let it go in a free fall, and the barrel slowly birled over with blue smoke trailing from its filling hole, enlacing the barrel with a blueish ribbon, like a rabbi winding the holy phylactery ribbons round his arm, and when the barrel stopped at the bottom, the assistant cooper took it, or sent it on its way with a kick, and the barrel came to rest on the slowly turning shafts of the rotary mechanism, one barrel alongside another, now all the barrels were turning and blueish smoke twisting round them like those circlets which bob round the heads of sanctified figures.

I watched, and as always when I watch work with fire, I got thirsty, my tongue stuck to my palate and instead of saliva I had nothing in my mouth but the like of cigarette papers. I raised the measure and received a shock, the pot practically shot up in the air, I had thought it still heavy with beer, but it was altogether light, because I had already drunk it all. The foreman squatted down and took the measure from me and laughed and went into the conditioning cellar, I knew he would draw me my beer with one pull, put a good top on it, maybe fill half the can with lager and finish it with dark garnet, a mixture that sends your body purring all over with approval. The Belgian geldings swished their fair tails like barley and whinnied, the drayman came out of the conditioning cellar bearing two cans, and gave one to each gelding, they took those cans in their teeth, pulled on the bridle and drank, as they drank they raised their necks high to let the very last drops of beer drain down their throats, and when they had finished, they tossed aside their cans and uttered a joyful neighing sound and pawed with their hooves and from their shoes pittered hardly visible sparks, the drayman laughed and nodded to me, I nodded back and the horses nodded too, the foreman squatted down and handed me the measure from the ramp, I sniffed at the foam and nodded, and Uncle Pepin began to sing, 'Oh ye lindens, o-o-oh ye li-i-inden trees!'

And the assistant cooper called out, 'Mr Josef, you know what a glorious day that will be when you sing Přemysl in the National Theatre?'

And Uncle Pepin nodded, stacking the barrels on to the sprayer of boiling pitch, tears dropped on to his apron, and the assistant cooper continued, 'And I warrant you this, when the first night comes, the folks from the brewery alone will make a whole busload to Prague, but you must keep training, now instead of the quarter we'll give you an empty half size on your chest.'

'A hectolitre, or a double if you like, long as it gets me up to the standard of Caruso and Mařáček,' Pepin shouted back.

'Half-and-half,' I told myself into the can and then I sipped in and gradually, holding back the desire to pour down the whole measure at once, ever so slowly and sweetly I swallowed down that light lager mixed with dark garnet, that half-and-half, *mutra* the maltsters called it, I drank ever so slowly and tenderly, just like when on a summer's early evening out there beyond the brewery, on the margins of the fields of rye, someone sits sweetly blowing a mournful song on the trombone, just for himself, with closed eyes and the tremor and quiver of the gleaming instrument in his brassy hands, just for its own sake till nightfall with his head leaning gently backwards, playing for himself his melancholic song.

The assistant cooper waved his hand over his head, 'And, Mr Josef, do you know who'll be in the box? Your brother and your sister-in-law, then Mr Jandák the mayor, that goes to the bars to check if the young ladies' calves are nice and firm as per regulation, what a pity your parents didn't live to see that day of glory, your mum and dad! What a joy it would've been!'

And Uncle Pepin wept, wiping the tears into his apron and nodding, and the assistant cooper went on mercilessly, 'Then after the performance the young ladies, Mr Josef, they would be throwing you bouquets of flowers and the newspaper men would be asking, where did you acquire all that talent, sir? And how would you answer them, Mr Josef, eh?'

'I'd say it was the gift of God,' cried Uncle Pepin pressing both hands to his face and weeping, and the barrels on the rotary mechanism turned and through its filling hole each barrel went on trailing out its tender saliva, which as each barrel rotated shaped around it a bobbing blueish circlet, a violet wheel, a neon necklace.

The assistant cooper went on triumphantly, 'But then you would have to tell the newspaper men, that your voice technique was learnt from a certain Austrian Captain von Meldík, that sang in the Vienna Opera House in his youth, that . . .'

And the assistant cooper didn't finish, Uncle roared and shook both his hands in the air, 'Balls! The Emperor wouldn't employ a tobacconist in the Opera, and if he did, only in the lavatories, and not even that. Just ye wait, Meldík, next time I pass the shop, I'll give ye a wee box in your window.'

The assistant cooper turned a barrel, held it, and the smoke rose up the cooper's chest and twined round his face, and the cooper called, 'Only Meldík said, the minute he spots you, he'll have the pepper ready, and as you bend over, he'll puff the pepper in your eyes, and then Meldík said . . .'

'Aye, what did he say, what?' roared Uncle Pepin.

'Mr Meldík said then he'd just run up and be able to do whatever he wants with you. Says he'll just give you a kick up the backside all the way back to the brewery,' the assistant cooper said daringly.

'What? And me an Austrian sodger, that was offered a rank and didna take it, me that carried the Captain's sabre? We'll soon see about that! Soon as I gets to the shop, over the bridge she goes, the whole jingbang into the Elbe!' shouted Uncle taking a barrel and heaving it up with his knee, and as he put it on the pin, the sprayer missed the opening and Uncle Pepin pressed on the foot lever and I put aside my measure of beer, laid it on the ramp and wiped my mouth, and at first I thought that the mixed lager with dark garnet must be making me see things, the assistant and the master cooper and the passing mechanic and old Řepa who was turning his shaft with a new lot of malt, all of them started to jig about and as they danced and capered they plucked at their cheeks and slapped their legs, they were like Moravian Slovaks dancing fancy figures, but old Řepa had to stay with his handle, so he went on turning the shaft, plucking at his face and alternately brandishing his hand and with the other turning the black globe, the drum in which the malt was roasting, till eventually, he tugged at the handle and shifted the drum away from the heat of the thirsty charcoal and like the coopers he jigged and capered, slapping his calves, as though being bitten by thousands of mosquitos.

The assistant cooper shouted, 'Mr Josef, turn off that pitch!'

And Uncle Pepin stamped his foot, but kept missing the spot, till finally he hit the lever, and only now did I see how, squirting from the spray nozzle in every direction, the tiny droplets of redhot pitch suddenly wilted, and all those delicate little thin amber tendrils, over which flew those little spatterings tiny as millet, or golden rice, or obtrusive insects, all these wands all at once sank into the dust of the brewery yard, and the coopers peeled off drying gobbets of pitch from their cheeks and the backs of their hands and necks and stared crossly at Uncle Pepin, as he stood there beside that huge stove that was still spluttering, hawking and belching thick short fire out of its bent chimney. Uncle Pepin knitted his scorched fingers and stared at the ground.

The master cooper said, 'Right, lads, it's back to work, so that Mr Josef here can get off soon to visit his young ladies.'

9

The new fashion began at the Hotel Na Knížecí. Soldiers brought in some apparatus, school headmasters assembled their pupils as early as six o'clock in the morning, and all the municipal corporations were involved, and as the day marched on through the great chamber there moved a line of curious participants, the soldiers put a kind of receiver, the sort telephones have, on every person's ear, and in that earpiece a crackling noise was heard and then some brass band music, which kept on playing the well-known tune *Koline, Koline*, but this music wasn't a bit beautiful, it was as if it was played on a long ago worn-out gramophone record, but all the same that music was being played in Prague and it was coming through the air, without wires, it was being drawn along like a thread and into the eye of the earpiece far away in our own little town. And everyone who heard it went out the back entrance of the hotel totally dazzled by this aural sensation, by the absence of any wire in bringing them Kmoch's Kolín Brass Band, and everybody walked past this queue of townspeople, this queue stretching right across the square as far as the main street, right down to Svoboda the baker's, and people who hadn't yet heard this wireless telegraphy, when they saw what blissful amazed expressions there were on the faces of those who had been granted a taste of this revolutionary new invention, all looked forward to it with greater and greater anticipation, as they approached in this procession winding into the Hotel Na Knížecí.

Mr Knížek, owner of the draper's shop, who liked making speeches, at once ordered his apprentice girl to bring the steps, then he got up on them and explained to the assembled citizenry, 'Good people, what you are about to hear is an invention, an appliance which our business party will strive to make available to every household, to every family in a year or two from now, at as reasonable a price as is feasible, so that every one of you can sit at home and receive not only music, but the news as well. I do not wish to anticipate, but this amenity can enable us to hear news not only from Prague, but maybe Brno too, music maybe even from Pilsen, and, to cast modesty completely to the winds, even news and music all the way from Vienna!' Mr Knížek declaimed from his stepladder.

Past that stepladder, with his handbarrow and assistant in tow, came Mr Zálaba, who delivered coal and wood about town, and when he heard Mr Knížek speaking, his assistant had to tip up the barrow, and Mr Zálaba ran up the rungs to the top of it and thundered and pointed at Mr Knížek, 'Look at him, the petty bourgeois! He thinks of nothing else but his huckster's decimal scales! Citizens, this invention is capable of establishing mutual understanding not only between towns, but also between nations, we welcome wireless telegraphy as the helpmate of the whole of humanity! For understanding among the peoples of all continents, all races, all nations!' Mr Zálaba declaimed, brandishing his arm in the air, and his assistant stood on the shaft of the barrow, but when he spotted a discarded fag-end on the pavement he couldn't resist and nipped over to pick it up, and the barrow tipped over and Mr Zálaba fell on to the paving stones, I only just avoided him.

And I hurried my bicycle home the minute I heard that foreshortened distance through the earphone between the brass-band music in Prague and my listening ear in the Hotel Na Knížecí. I took off my skirt, laid it on the table, picked up the scissors, and at the point where the knees come in the skirt, I cut short the material, producing so much left-over cloth that I reckoned my dressmaker could make me a bolero out of it, and instantly I took a needle and bound the new edge, and almost feverishly I pulled the skirt on and went straight over to look in the mirror, and there I saw it! Ten years younger I was for that foreshortening of distances. I turned round and knew at once that of course the garters had to be much higher up, and then I saw for an absolute certainty that only now were my legs really beautiful, those beautiful shadows in the tendons under the knees, those brown imprints of God's thumb, were capable of arousing much surprise and delight, but also much civic indignation, especially from Francin, who, when he saw me like this, would blush to the roots of his hair and declare that no decent woman ever wore a skirt like that. And I ran out into the yard and jumped on my bike and rode out of the brewery to the Cross, such a pleasurable draught wafted round my knees, reaching up to my garters, I could pedal much more freely in that trimmed skirt, the only thing that bothered me was, I had to cycle with one hand on the handlebars, with the other I had to keep pulling my skirt down all the time, as it rode up my legs with the motion of my knees. And now out of the Hořátev turning Mr Kropáček came on his Hendee 'Indian' motorbike, as always he was sitting in the sidecar and steering the motorcycle with one leg slung over the handlebars and one hand controlling the gas on the end of one of the bars, I liked to watch him start the bike up in the brewery, the minute he got going he climbed across from the saddle into the sidecar, tossed out one leg as if out of the bath, and then he drove on comfortably home. So now, Mr Kropáček, when he caught sight of my bare knees at the turning in the road, he clean missed the corner and drove off into the cherry orchard, and I took that as a good omen and hurried on across the bridge, only slowing down outside the Hotel Na Knížecí. Slowly I rode past that queue waiting to experience the new invention, on the subject of which Headmaster Kupka had declared, 'I don't know, I really don't know, but it bodes nobody any good,' and everybody sort of stopped focusing on what was awaiting them in the Hotel Na Knížecí, and concentrated on my knees, and shortened skirt, all of them stopped looking at the hotel entrance and turned in my direction. Headmaster Kupka pointed his umbrella at me and said to the Dean, 'And there you have it, the first results!' But the Dean bowed to me and said, 'A lady's full genuflection is another name for the Holy Spirit.' And I stopped outside the cake shop, before putting my little shoe on the pavement I drew back my hair so that it wouldn't get tangled in the spokes, I leant the bicycle against the wall, and as I went down the pavement I felt as if I was walking along in a bathing suit.

And in the cake shop I ordered Mr Navrátil to wrap me four cream horns, and I took one right away and leant forward to stop the flaky pastry getting in my blouse. And again, as I crammed the cream horn voraciously into my mouth, at once I heard Francin's voice saying that no decent woman would eat a cream puff like that, and Mr Navrátil smiled guardedly, because he had no teeth, and I paused in front of the window display, just let the women see my silhouetted profile from inside the dark shop, and Mr Navrátil handed me a small parcel done up with blue string. I paid, and Mr Navrátil opened the door for me, and before I rode off, he helped me with my hair, running alongside the bike for a bit, till the hair got into the airstream. I pedalled off with all my might, steering with one hand and holding that delicious parcel on one finger, and my hair welled up behind me, just like those beautiful brass balls in the regulator of a steam traction engine when it's revving up. I went on making as if to look at the middle of the road in front of me, but on both pavements I could see all the various kinds of human eyes, those admiring eyes as well as those glances full of hatred for my bare knees, as they rose up alternately like camshaft joints . . .

And when I reached the brewery I rode at once over to the stables, Mutzek ran to meet me, good little doggie, he wagged his long tail, and when I bent down to him he licked my palm and half-closed his eyes, and I went into the shed and brought an axe and unwrapped the parcel and offered Mutzek a cream puff, and he was distrusting at first, but when I laughed he started eating the cream puff and I considered in my mind how much I ought to take off to shorten Mutzek's tail, and I placed the chopping block behind Mutzek and took his tail and laid it on the block, but Mutzek turned round, so I stroked him and offered him another cream puff, and Mutzek, his paw mucky with whipped cream, licked my hand and the axe-handle too and tucked into the second cream puff, and I laid out Mutzek's tail on the block, and then with one blow I chopped off the greater part of it and Mutzek gasped, he had half of the cream puff inside him, but the pain in his tail was doubtless so great, that Mutzek started to moan and turn around and with his mouth full of sugary foam he took hold of the stump of his tail, out of which blood was dripping, and Mutzek thought someone else had done it, not me, he licked my hand and the remains of his tail by turns, I stroked him and comforted him, 'Mutzy dear, it'll only last a short moment, think how handsome and beautiful you'll be, it's the fashion, it has to be like this, take a look and see!' I straightened up and showed him how my skirt was shortened too, but Mutzek began to lament dreadfully and I could see that I hadn't chopped quite enough off, I ought to chop off just another little piece, but Mutzek wouldn't hear of any continuation, I held his tail down on the block, I promised him all the cream puffs, and said I would buy him some more, but Mutzek broke free and took the chopped off piece of tail into his little mouth and ran off with it to the office, and just as the draymen were coming out, he ran into the counting house.

A moment later Francin rushed out of the office, in one hand he held a number three lettering pen, in the other that piece of tail, and Mutzek stood on the last step and barked in the direction of the shed and stables, out of which I was just wheeling my bike, and when I rode up in front of the office, Doctor Gruntorád came bowling along into the brewery. The chairman's stallion had had its tail cropped and its mane trimmed and the doctor jumped down from the driving seat, tossed the reins to the coachman, and taking a look at my skirt he proclaimed, 'Everything is going to have to be shortened and there's no end to what is needed. So, manager, now we're going to shorten the working week, from the first of the month Saturdays will be cut by half, so we'll knock off at twelve. The distances to landlords will be shortened by driving out to them. We'll sell your Orion motorbike and get you a motor-car, which will shorten the time taken up and make scope for a greater turnover of beer. Ivan!' cried Doctor Gruntorád at the coachman. 'Hand me my first-aid box, let's put some plasters on the little doggie to stop that bleeding.'

That afternoon Francin took the Orion off to Prague. I took the opportunity and after work I went off to the lodgings to see Uncle Pepin. Under a lit bulb Uncle Pepin was brandishing his fist at a great huge maltster, who was kneeling, but even on his knees he was still the same size as Uncle Pepin standing, but Uncle put on a threatening face and roared out, 'Suppose I canna hold myself back! Suppose I just fetches you a mighty great Ostrava miner's clout with my fist!'

And the great enormous maltster clasped his hands and begged him, 'Oh, Mr Josef, don't make a widow of me wife and orphans of me children!'

And the other maltsters standing round in a circle laughed quietly to themselves, those who couldn't stand it any longer ran out into the corridor and stood there facing the wall and drumming their fists against the plaster and drowning in fits of laughter. And when they had finished choking they ran back into the lodgings.

And Uncle Pepin stood legs astride beneath the light bulb and cried out, 'So let's have you the now!'

And he threw himself at the huge maltster, who gave ground, and Uncle Pepin gave him a half-nelson, and tried to put him to the floor, but the maltster reared up and knocked Uncle over and pinned him down and everyone around shouted and clapped, but Uncle Pepin grabbed him round the neck and the maltster allowed himself to be turned just about almost on to his back, but at the last minute he knelt and Uncle gave him a full nelson and the maltster stood up and walked round the room with Uncle, carrying Uncle like a little child, but Uncle Pepin yelled out in his delight, 'And it's a stunning victory, just like our own Gustav Frištenský!'

Then the maltster knelt again and did a somersault with Uncle, only now did I notice that the two wrestlers were wearing white long-johns, right down to their ankles and tied at the ankle with laces. And as the huge maltster did the somersault, he pinned Uncle Pepin down, lay on his head, but Uncle shouted out, 'Give up, it's no use, I've got ye held fast!'

But the great huge maltster reared up, nabbed Uncle Pepin by the ankles and neck and set him spinning and then fell over with him, but Uncle Pepin roared out, 'That's set ye flying, like Frištenský that time with the negro!'

And then the maltster weakened and Uncle Pepin took him by the shoulders and the maltster subsided into laughter and laughed till the tears, ran, and Uncle put him on the floor and the chief maltster knelt down and announced, 'Mr Josef, you're the winner again!'

And the wrestlers stood up, Uncle bowed and smiled, bowing at the throngs which only he could see around him.

'And tomorrow it's the return bout,' said the chief maltster and dipped his face in his can.

'Uncle Jožin,' I said, 'could you come over to us for a minute and lend us your saw, please?'

And Uncle Pepin recovered his breath, nodded his head, then he went over and threw the blanket off his bunk, all his underwear and other clothes were at the foot of it, he rolled aside the bolster, which was all grimy at the head, and under the bolster he had all sorts of little boxes and reels of thread and so many funny useless tiny bits and bobs, here Uncle found a key, opened his cupboard and pulled out of it a paper bag, upon which was written: *Alois Šisler, Hatter and Furrier*, and out of that bag he took a beautiful white sailor's cap with golden cords and the gold-embroidered emblem *Viribus Unitis*.

'Old Šisler sewed me this, he wouldn't have done it for anyone else but me!' So saying he planted that beautiful white sailor's cap on his head, and there he stood in his long-johns, behind him the tumbled bed with its kicked underwear and clothing at the foot and its load of useless funny old things at the head.

'Uncle Jožin,' I said, 'that's a lovely bed you've got there, I'll sew you some covers for it, alright?'

'If ye want,' said Uncle, quickly getting dressed.

And the maltsters stood round and watched, they gazed at the floor and couldn't manage to say me a single word, they even seemed sorry that I'd turned up in the middle of all that fun with Uncle Pepin, because it was their fun and I didn't belong in it, between me and them lay a difference like the one between this lodging room, where eight of them sleep together, and my three rooms and kitchen, where I sleep and Francin, the brewery manager, who may even make it one day to brewery director, while they will still only be maltsters, till the day they retire, the day they die. Uncle Pepin closed the cupboard and glowed with joy over that cap, the kind only sea captains wear, or first officers.

'Good night to you, sirs,' I said and went out of the lodgings.

Before we had pushed through the gust of wind at the corner of the maltings, the light bulbs began to quaver at the corners of the brewery and stables, as if the draught was draining the electricity out of them. Uncle's cap glowed like the milky shade of a paraffin lamp and Uncle had to hold on to that cap tight with both hands to stop the buffets of wind whipping it away from him. It even seemed to me as if Uncle Pepin was just about to float up in the air like once my bouclé bathtowel did . . . and I knew for a cert that Uncle Pepin wouldn't give up his cap, that he'd rather fly zig-zag up into the darkness towards the brewery chimneys and gyrating weathervanes. And when I lit the lamps and Uncle brought the saw over from the master cooper, I knocked over a chair and Uncle and I shortened the legs of the chair, not much, by ten centimetres, which each time I measured with a tailor's tape-measure. When we laid the table on its side, Uncle Pepin said, 'Sister-in-law, do ye know what? What's the point of measuring it all with that tape-measure? Let's just saw off one leg and then lay the sawn-off block against the next leg, and then we can just saw them off straight without measuring.'

I gave a laugh, 'Uncle Pepin, you ought to have joined the police force, with such brains!'

And Uncle Pepin shouted, 'You leave the police out of this! Uncle Adolf had only been with the force just a month, straight off they took him with them in hot pursuit of one particular character, surrounded the building he was in, and when they entered the kitchen there was his other half sitting all by herself and the chief detective says, "Where's your old man?" And she says, "Gone to cut tree stumps," and the chief kicks in the door to the living-room and there through the open window he sees this character darting up the hillside, so he orders them, "After him!" And Adolf is first out the window, lands up to his neck in manure, but he scrambles up out of it and off they all scamper into the woods waving a revolver and there they had the character surrounded, and he had a revolver too, so they were persuading him to chuck it away, and the character said if they took one step further he was going to shoot, and so the commander spent an hour persuading the character, saying he'd get mitigating circumstances and guaranteeing him personally only six months, and so the character chucked away his revolver, and triumphantly the commander put the handcuffs on him and they led him off to the bus, and Adolf wanted to get into the police vehicle too, but they said that with all that manure on him he couldn't, so he had to go on foot all the way to the very outskirts of Ostrava, and there they threw him off the tram, so he had to walk all the way home on foot, and at home the landlady wouldn't take his clothes for the wash, so he carted them off to the cleaners and took his ticket, and when he came back a fortnight later to get his clothes, there was heaps of folk around and lots of lassies he knew too, and when Adolf's turn in the queue came the manageress took his ticket, and when she came back, she was all red in the face and she threw the parcel back at Adolf and yelled at him, "Ye've shat yersel', haven't ye, so ye can just go and wash it yersel'!" And he went home all shamefaced . . .'

And so Uncle went on and I smiled and we sawed the legs off the table according to Pepin's recipe, we shortened the table height by ten centimetres, and Uncle Pepin said, 'And so Adolf had no luck in life, once he was passing this pub, and some drunken dentists were there, and they invited Adolf for a drink, and when he'd had some and was glad folks were being nice to him again, all of a sudden one dentist in a drunken stupor pulled out another dentist's front teeth, and seeing as Adolf was drunk too, the one that pulled out the front teeth took Adolf and pulled out all his back teeth, mind you Adolf was dead lucky there was no drunken gelders around that night . . .'

'That would've been pretty mighty sore,' I said, laying a sawn-off piece to the last leg and we went on sawing merrily away and Uncle Pepin expatiated, 'But then they took Adolf off on military exercises and he was right over in Turčanský Svätý Martin and again, seeing as Uncle Adolf was a qualified engine-driver, they gave him a Sentinel to drive, and one day this bloke, sergeant-major, was reading the army paper and he finds in the circulars, steam-roller needed for road surfacing outside barracks, Cheb, so he gives Adolf his orders and ration allowances, and Uncle Adolf sets off for Cheb in his Sentinel following his map, this was in the spring, and Adolf spent the whole summer just going westwards across Slova-kia, and in the autumn he crossed the Moravian border and went on his way, but slower and slower, because each Sunday he went off home, and when he'd spent all autumn getting through Moravia, he went back to make discreet enquiries at the barracks in Turčanský Svätý Martin, but there they told him the sergeant-major had hanged himself, because a gun had been found on the square and nobody knew who put it there, so they had stuck it in the stores and that was one gun too many, and so Adolf went on his way in the Sentinel right across the length of Czechoslovakia, and by spring he'd got as far west as Pilsen, but as he hadn't any coal he had to stoke the boiler up with firewood, begging and borrowing on the road, but he burned up an awful lot of folk's fences too, spe-cially when he was a long way off from the woods, and he was terribly delayed, as in fact he was only driving the Sentinel one day at a time in the end, because it took him three days to get home to Ostrava for the Sunday, and three days travelling back to the Senti-nel again, and so finally in the summer Uncle Adolf made it to the garrison in Cheb, and there they locked the pair of them up, Adolf and the Sentinel, and when it was all sorted out and explained, they sent Uncle Adolf as military watch to Košumberk Castle, and as he had nowhere to go now, there out of boredom at Košumberk he fell in love with the daughter of the visitors' guide, and he married her, and all that time he stood there on guard, toting his weapon, but after three years of this he reckoned they'd likely forgotten him, so he just stripped off his uniform, stashed his weapon away in a corner, and there he is to this day, working as a visitors' guide . . .' and Uncle Pepin straightened himself as the last block of wood dropped off.

I took the lamp and carried it across to the sideboard, to see how this table was going to look shortened by ten centimetres. And when Uncle and I put the overturned table on its side I stared wide-eyed with astonishment and my eyes just popped. I went through to the kitchen, stood for a while on the doorstep and gazed out over the orchard treetops at the brewery chimney stack, then after a bit I went back in.

Uncle Pepin was knitting his fingers.

'What's to be done? Nothing's to be done, Uncle Jožin,' I told him,'bring me over those historical novels of Beneš Třebízský from the bookcase, would you?'

And I righted the table, that table off whose legs in half-darkness Uncle Pepin and I had sawn four times ten centimetres, but each time we'd gone and placed the ten-centimetre block against one and the same leg, hadn't we, so that we'd shortened this one leg by forty centimetres . . . and Uncle Pepin brought along those old historical novels and I piled them under the missing leg, but it wasn't enough, so I had to finish it off with Šmilovský's *Parnassia*.

Away in the distance a clatter and thunder resounded, that was Francin on his Orion just coming out of the little woods near Zvěřínek, and that din and clamour grew ever stronger and louder, as if Francin were bulldozing all the Orion's dismantled parts along in front of him. I ran out in front of the office and opened the gates, and Francin rode into the brewery, swaying about on the sidecar was the little lathe which Francin always took with him on longer excursions, and now the motorbike swerved to our front door, and Francin raised his goggles and removed his leather helmet and motioned with his hand for me to go back quick into the house, and I knew he'd brought me another little gift. I ran into the kitchen, and Francin came dragging something in through the back, across the office passage and into the living room, for a while he fiddled with something in there and then he came into the kitchen rubbing his hands and laughing, he patted Uncle Pepin on the shoulder and I threw myself at Francin and as was our custom searched through all his coat pockets and in his trousers, and Francin laughed and was quite charming, till I was altogether tantalized, what could be behind all this? And then I said, 'So it's not a little ring or some earrings, and it's not a watch or a little brooch, it's something bigger, isn't it?' And Francin took off his coat and washed his hands and nodded his head, and as he was drying his hands I pointed to the door into the living room and asked, 'Is it in there?' Francin nodded that it was . . . and was purposely slow in getting changed and purposely pretended he had to polish his shoes, till I threatened to burst into the room, because I couldn't stand it any longer. Francin raised a finger, asked me to close my eyes, and led me off into the room, and there he let me stand a while, and then I heard music, a tenor began to sing most beautifully . . . 'For you my heart is cryin', white flower, my Hawaii . . .' I opened my eyes, turned, and Francin stood holding the burning lamp and shining it on a box gramophone, then he placed the lamp on the table and asked me for a dance, caught me round the waist, squeezing my palm with his other hand, and then Francin paused till the right moment, and finally swam with a long step into . . . 'And though he say farewell dear, yet he'll return to you here . . .' and Francin, I was amazed, because he was a poor dancer, he swam into the steps of the tango so well, that I pressed myself to him, he insinuated his leg altogether quite boldly between mine, we were so nicely dovetailed I drew back to get a better look at Francin, then I laid my head on his shoulder, but there came a turn in the dance and Francin slipped out of rhythm. He waited a moment, and when he tried to continue the tango by gliding backwards, he glided correctly, but out of rhythm, and he lost confidence, but when he let the whole thing slide and paused till those first three steps came round, he picked up the thread and swam beautifully across the carpet and avoided twirling about this time, he didn't even want to step away from me, but with long strides, as if his shoes were stuck in hot asphalt, he simply danced from one end of the room to the other, turning awkwardly and stepping out again in rhythm, and yet he couldn't resist trying another turn, he moved away from me and scrutinized his steps on the carpet, I could see those steps were correct, but Francin was lacking one vital thing: the rhythm. He even had a go at flinging me over backwards, it flashed through my head he must have been going to ballroom dancing classes, some private dancing school in Prague, because he even did that trick to perfection, he bent me over backwards till my hair touched the carpet, but when he drew me back towards him, that was correct too, but all the time the thread of the dancing steps was missing the eye of the musical needle . . . and the beautiful tenor stopped singing and the music quietly subsided . . . and Francin stopped smiling and practically collapsed on to a chair, and his inability to get the tango right, his consciousness of failure left him gasping for breath, because at the last masked ball I had danced with young Klečka, a brewster at the brewery, who played the cello beautifully and had four classes of technical school and knew how to dance, and he and I by mutual agreement, when the other dancers had stopped and gathered round us, we two danced together like two true artistes, like two coupled axles, in pure symbiosis, while Francin sat alone behind a pillar and gazed at the floor.

'When I'm with Miss Vlasta at Havrda's,' said Uncle Pepin, 'we dance too, only a wee bit different, faster than that, Vlasta pours me a Martell and then she says, "Well Mr Josef, what can I play for you today?" And I says, "Give us a good belter!" And Vlasta says, "You what? Which one?" And I says, "By the composer Bunda, known as Gobelinek," so may I have the pleasure also, sister-in-law? Francin, make it go quite a good bit faster! And get a load of this real dancing!'

Uncle Pepin took me by the hands and the jazzy music started to play so fast, with Francin shifting the speed lever forward, like women rushing about in a speeded-up film. And Uncle Pepin began to bow to me and I bowed to him too. Then he touched me with his forehead, and I him, suddenly Uncle turned to the rhythm of the music, and keeping a hold of each other's hands, we turned about to stand back to back to each other, and Uncle lifted a foot and twisted and waggled his shoe and calf, then he spread his arms, clapped his palms and revolved his hands as fast as if he were swiftly winding wool, then he crooked his hands at his waist and cut with his feet this way and that, so that I had to do the same, but the opposite way, so as he wouldn't kick my ankles, then he turned and took me by the waist and tossed me up to the ceiling, till I touched the plaster with my hair, and then Uncle carried me hither and thither to the rhythm of the music, with his nose buried in my navel, then he let me go, turned me round and back to back we touched each other, and Uncle heaved me up on his shoulders like a bundle and I locked myself in his shoulders like a bundle and I locked myself in his arms too, and we rocked each other to and fro, as if straightening strains in the smalls of our backs, then Uncle let me go, ran round me in a rhythmic trot and started lunging at me, like the Knave of Hearts with his pikestaff, I copied him, and the dance was exact and elusive, but constantly rhythmic, as if the motion filled out the music much more exactly than any other form of dance, then Uncle leapt up and spreadeagled his legs and landed on the carpet and did the splits, and I was afraid I might rupture my groin, so I merely bowed left and right, while Uncle sniffed alternately at his left toecap and his right, then all of a sudden, as if suctioned up to the ceiling, he jumped up, drew his legs together and pulled me so niftily up on to his shoulder, then over his shoulder feet first and down on to the ground again, that I made a stroke mark on the ceiling with the heel of my shoe. Francin watched me smilingly, then he went to the kitchen and came back holding in one hand a mug of warm white coffee and in the other a slice of dry bread, which he nibbled away at, and he watched us, but the speeded-up tango was fading away, the tenor drew to an end . . .' And though he say farewell dear, yet he'll return to you here . . . white flower, my Hawaii, I dream of you . . .' And as Uncle Pepin led me off the dance floor, he kissed my hand and held my arm and bowed deeply on all sides, bowing to some great ballroom and sending kisses out to all corners of the room . . . And just as I walked past the table, I trod on one of the little sawn-off blocks from the leg and sprained my ankle.

'Brother,' said Francin, 'harmony hibernates within you.'

And I fell with a shout and couldn't get up again.

During that night Mutzek took leave of his senses. In the evening the caretaker had had to chain him up in the shed, and there Mutzek was unable to sort out in his mind the relationship between cream puffs and the pain in his tail, and also he didn't want to be a hand-some young fellow in the latest fashion, and so he began to howl dreadfully and foam appeared at his mouth, the foam of insanity mixed with the foam of cream puffs, and at midnight Francin loaded his Browning pistol and went out into the yard, and after a while I heard firing, one shot after another, I hobbled to the window and saw in the light of an electric torch Mutzek straining at his chain, standing on his hind legs and begging with his paws, agree-ing to the shortened tail, reconciled to all, as long as his loving master didn't shoot, and Francin fired off a whole round, but Mutzek still did not drop, on the contrary, he was more moving than ever before, he kept standing up on his hind legs and waggling his front paws, and I took it all as a mortal sin which I had inflicted on Mutzek, and I hobbled to the ottoman and burst into tears and jammed up my ears to avoid hearing those shots like accusations ... And the firing stopped, and I expect Mutzek was dead by now, but surely up to the last moment he had gone on wagging his non-existent tail, because he probably thought someone else was shooting him, since as an animal he surely didn't and couldn't have understood how we could cause him this pain, I and his loving master, Francin, who, when he returned with his Browning, rolled dressed as he was into bed and it seemed to me that he was crying too.

Now Francin had me the way he wanted me to be, a nice decent woman sitting at home, he knew where this woman was, and where she would be tomorrow, somewhere he would like to make her stay for always, not too ill, but sort of ailing, a woman who would hobble to the stove, to the chair, to the table, but above all a woman who would be some kind of a burden, because for Francin it was the height of matrimonial bliss when I was grateful to him for making me my breakfast in the morning, and going on the motorbike at midday to fetch lunch from the restaurant, but above all it meant he could show me how much he loved me, with what joy he was prepared to care for me, and somehow, just as he took care of me, so ought I to be taking care of him, that was Francin's dream, that every year I might catch angina and flu, and occasionally even get pneumonia. That always made him blissfully happy, nobody else knew how to look after a person like Francin did, that was his religion, his heaven on earth, when he could wrap me in sheets dampened in cold water, when he ran round me with the sheet and wound it on to me as if he were embalming me alive, but then he took me in his arms and laid me carefully in my bed, like little girls do with their dolls. And once an hour he dashed out of the office to take my temperature, every two hours he changed my compresses, praying no doubt in his heart, not that he would wish it, but if Fate would not decree otherwise, that I should never get up from my bed, so that I could be his little child, who needed him just as much as he needed me. And when I was convalescing and starting to get about, when I began inwardly to laugh again, and again that indecent woman in me started to get the upper hand, Francin withdrew into himself and dreamt again about me being paralysed and him pushing me in a wheelchair, in the evening he would read to me from the *National Politics* daily or a novel, and this would assuage his complex about my rude state of health, which loved chance and the unexpected happening and the marvellous encounter, whereas Francin loved order and regularity, repetition indicated to him the right path in life, everything that could be predicted and fixed, that was Francin's existence, a world he believed in and without which he could not have lived.

And now he had me in bed with my ankle bandaged in glowing plaster, immobile for a long time to come, and if and when, at first on crutches and then with a walking stick, now, while Josephine Baker dances the Charleston.

And maybe my ankle came along in the nick of time because while I was running about Francin was incapable of putting together a single advertising slogan, he covered so many quarter slips of paper with his number three lettering pen, and all that advertising for increased turnover of beer ended up in the stove. Now however, with my white leg resting on its cushion, Francin walked up and down the kitchen and living room, drank lukewarm coffee and nibbled at a piece of dry bread, and suddenly he stopped short with the mug in his hand, as though in a dream, assailed even by a vision, which made him squint. He put aside the mug and the bread, sat himself down, and the number three lettering pen wrote out calligraphic notices for the pubs, and when he had finished, he took a drawing pin and fastened each quarter sheet of paper to the wall, so that I could see it, so that I might get the message, that if only I was healthy but behaved as if I was ill, any day now he would be appointed director of the brewery, that limited-liability company, such zest for work and life my paralysed mobility gave him. In a week Francin must have drunk for inspiration at least half a hundred litres of lukewarm white coffee and across the whole wall he hung out the graphically decorative slogans he had created with his lettering pen. – Drink more ale, for fewer aches and woes. – Our fine ale, reinforcement for flagging constitutions. – Without his glass he sighed alas, after his beer he flushed like a lass and made good cheer. – Without my ale in living death I'd wail. – Our fine ale, reinforcement and fortification of flagging constitutions. – Drink more beer, make better cheer. – Hearty, fresh and hale, you'll find good health in our ale. – If you wish to have good cheer, come along and drink our beer. – They who fraternize the tavern, live a life of double heaven. – Our wholesome beer, the drink for everyone. – Live a life of better cheer, come along and drink more beer. – Who shuns the tavern with his feet, who does not drink and does not eat, his health he surely will defeat. – At home, on your journey, beer is always refreshing. – Beer at every time and tide, beer refreshes your inside. And he was so pleased by his bout of inspiration, he poured himself a full mug of coffee, and put on the gramophone . . . 'Far away across the sea, lies a magic land, Hawaii . . .' and he tried with creeping steps to dance the tango, and being so brimful of optimism, and so happy about some event lying in the near future, in the evening he locked himself up in the living room, and played *White Flower, My Hawaii*, over and over again. Every other while he came out holding a modern dance manual and laughing, and when he'd expressed his delight, he returned again to the room, the key hole shone into the half-darkness just like my leg in plaster, and I knew that Francin must have drawn all the steps with chalk, in footprints, not only the basic steps, but also the steps backward, the turns, a whole itinerary of chalk-marked outlines of shoe soles, which he patiently paced through, in the rhythm and melody of *Hawaii*. He was so happy that he was managing the steps now that even in the daytime, when I was looking out the window into the yard and Francin was in a hurry to take instructions to the brewing house, suddenly he would slow down and pace out the steps of the tango, then turn around and backwards, with his arms slightly raised, he would continue this modern dancing, I saw him looking at his feet, I saw he was confounded, that if he could, he would chalk out those dance steps on the road . . . but that didn't put him off, on the contrary, that evening he tried all the more fervently to pinpoint on the chalk-marked carpet that little chink through which he might enter truly into the rhythm of the gramophone, as it performed

Hawaii for the hundredth time. Every evening Francin removed the electric battery from his Orion motorcycle, brought it in and switched on the high-frequency currents, the case padded with red velvet gleamed dimly with its glassy instruments, and Francin put sparks in my ankle, fulgurational flashes penetrated the plaster bandaging, then he removed my items of clothing one by one, without my realizing I was practically naked, the fulgurational currents made me feel good, the massage roller with its tiny sparklets fortified both my legs and reinforced the nerves in my spine, and Francin whispered to me, 'The best method, Mary, of enhancing your beauty, using fulgurational currents to conserve the beauty you have now . . .' I looked forward every evening to these violet massagings, with the scent of thunder and short circuits, across the orchard you could hear again the lovely male voice, Mr Jirout in his little satin suit, firing himself with his voice from a cannon, through the wall I could see him fly over the brewery, hands by his sides and smiling a crinkly smile . . . 'the love that was, it is gone, 'twas for but a short while . . . golden lassie . . .' and now Mr Jirout began to veer towards the ground, he spread his arms and cast roses and kisses to the watchers below, Francin put a metal electrode in my hand and turned on the machine with a black knob and like a hypnotist he hovered with his palm over my body, wherever Francin's hand moved, there sparks sizzled and crackled from his palm, raining down a shower of purple violet grain, thousands of forget-me-nots and violets from Francin's palm entered me from this appliance, the scent of ozone and lightning striking the building hovered over me, even the ankle dipped in plaster glowed with a blueish sheen . . . 'her life is o'er . . . to the deep linn by Nymburk town she's gone . . .' and Mr Jirout landed in the trampoline net and bounced and bowed in his little blue satin suit . . . I felt my body too emitting its own pungent scent of electricity, I was breathing more and more heavily, my whole body radiated its own halo, I looked at myself in the mirror, lying stretched out, the purple violet crackle and sizzle my only camisole, I never had the sense that I was naked, all the time I was encased in a periwinkle coat, and Francin's gutta-percha collar and white shirt cuffs shone just like my plaster leg, he was breathing just like me, lying on my back with my elbow crooked over my eyes. I used to feel all funny from that high-frequency ritual, Francin and I never used to talk about it, we prepared in silence, as if both of us were striving for something forbidden, and when Francin turned back the black knob, each time we avoided each other's eyes, so beautiful it was. If someone had suddenly burst into the room bearing a lamp, Francin would certainly have fainted, and so he preferred to lock the door, draw the blinds and curtain, and for safety's sake he went out and looked in at the windows, to make sure no one could peep in at us and see him unbuttoning my blouse with quivering fingers, drawing the skirt down carefully over the plaster ankle, kneeling down in front of me and reaching out with this cosmetic massage to the cosmos.

Today Dr Gruntorád came, he asked me to make him some strong tea, saying he'd caught a chill in the night from attending mothers in labour, he drew his scissors out of his bag, and while he was cutting my plaster bandage he sneezed a couple of times, then fell asleep in the middle of cutting, with the scissors still in his fingers, and he was so deeply asleep, I couldn't resist, I pulled out his gold watch from his waistcoat pocket, looked to see what time it was, and quietly slipped the watch back in its place, so carefully and so thrilled by the precision of my movements, and in that pickpocketing escapade I was once more my old self, the clock on the wall showed me what time it was, but I just wanted to test myself, to see if I hadn't lost my pluck, to see if I was still capable of doing whatever I fancied, and yes, things weren't too bad after all. I used to go to Mr Pollak's drapery shop to buy buttons just because in the afternoon nobody used to be around in the shop, and as Mr Pollak bent down beneath the counter to fetch a box, I would stretch my hand across the counter and take a child's fake watch, and when Mr Pollak straightened up, I would look all innocent, and in his eyes I could read that he was quite oblivious of my theft, and when I asked to see some more buttons and Mr Pollak bent down, quickly I hung the watch back, and when Mr Pollak straightened up, I smiled, I grew up taller somehow inside, and with that theft and its immediately ensuing effective repentance I released tension, breathed my relief, and on going out of the shop I felt as if I had sprouted wings so great that I was scraping the door frame with them and feathers were fluttering off me, which Mr Pollak had to sweep up kneeling with a shovel . . . and Dr Gruntorád sneezed

and woke up and finished cutting my bandage, which split open
like a white casing, then the doctor felt my ankle over, declaring,
'Now you can get up to your mischief again . . .' and he sneezed and
I took my crutches and brought a mug of tea, and when I tried to
put my weight on my leg it collapsed under me and I said, 'It doesn't
even feel like my own leg!' and Dr Gruntorád said, 'It's your leg
all right, you'll be right as rain in a week . . . tishoo!' he sneezed
with feeling. 'Doctor,' I said, 'I'm breathing a bit funny too.' 'Take
off your blouse if you would,' said the doctor, taking a sip of his tea.
Then he laid his ear on my back, and as always that ear was cold, as
if he were laying a small glass ashtray on me, the warmer the
weather, the colder his ear was, he tapped my back, asked me to
breathe deeply, and then his index finger tapped on my back, lightly
he touched my back with his ear, like boys putting their ears to
telegraph poles, I flicked the current of my hair over, and the doctor fell asleep again, buried in my hair, as if asleep on a bench
beneath a weeping willow tree. Once I went past Dr Gruntorád's villa specially on purpose to see if that willow tree was
actually there, overshadowing the whole house, it was such a long
time ago I supposed since his wife used to receive visits from a
colonel gent who came from Brandejs on horseback, and Dr Gruntorád, then young and undoubtedly stalwart, unexpectedly
returned home in the night, grabbed his gun in passing on the
ground floor and went up and kicked open the door to his wife's
bedroom, just in time to glimpse the colonel dashing to the open
first-floor window. He managed to take aim, and as the colonel pro-
pelled himself from the window sill with a clatter and plunged
headlong out into the depths of night and down into the faded lilac
bushes and flowering jasmines, Dr Gruntorád managed to scatter
buckshot at the colonel's vanishing topboots and another load
merely at the stars of the blue night filling the empty window
frame . . . I would often wake in the night with this image, which
kept me awake, I could never properly imagine and associate this
wonderful incident with the person of Dr Gruntorád, I kept connecting it in my mind with somebody else, but a quite tangible
image connected me with the colonel gent, who with his topboot

shot through still managed to hop up on his horse, managed to pull a stem of willow out of his boot, lean from his horse right down to the ground and stick that stem in the ground, a stem which today has become such a huge willow tree, that in stormy and windy nights it taps against the window panes of the whole house like a living memorial. And Dr Gruntorád continued tapping his index finger on my back, maybe he wasn't even aware he'd previously dropped off, he tapped away like a miner buried in the pit, and when he turned round he took a sip of tea, and while I was dressing, he quietly wrote out his prescription, and again his golden fountain pen suddenly halted, for a few seconds Dr Gruntorád dropped off, then he woke again and feeling revived finished writing out the prescription of medicine for my chest. I said to him, 'Doctor, has my husband boasted to you yet about something he bought for me?' 'Show me!' instructed the doctor and sipped his tea. I opened the case lying there on the table. 'What kind of junk is that? Where did the fellow buy it?' said the doctor. I said to him, 'In Prague, but seeing as you've got a cold, here's a really beautiful attachment, a bit like our national anthem, pines rustle on the rocky slopes.' The doctor said, 'And do you know how to operate it?' I said, 'Doctor, there's nothing to it . . . Look!' and I plugged it in and twisted the black knob and fitted on the tube with bristles for the nerves, and purple violet sawdust sizzled from the bristles, and the doctor ran his fingers down his knuckles and smiled naively and said, 'It's poetical, it can't do anybody any harm, and coming from you, it'll be a pleasure . . .' And I took the electrode, the ozone inhalator and atomizer, and I told him, 'Doctor, the best thing would be if you could lie down on the ottoman . . .' The doctor sat down on the settee, I drew the beige curtain, and the sprinkled half-darkness and the little purple violet bush of electric discharges sizzling from that special electrode for the nerves, gave a glow to the doctor's bald pate, as he lowered himself gently on to the ottoman. Now he lay on his back, holding in his fingers that constantly sputtering and crackling wand, while I prepared the ozone inhalator with its atomizer. Into the wadding of the ozone inhalator I put some drops of eucalyptus oil with menthol essence, screwed into the tube the forked glass attachment, for sticking into your nose, and then I took the little nerve brush away from the doctor and stuck into the cathode that ozone inhalator with its atomizer and turned the wheel, and the hollow tube filled with neon gas, which percolated through the wadding, soaked in eucalyptus oil. I knelt in front of the settee and put the appliance gently close up to the doctor's nostrils. I told him, 'This is bound to cure you, doctor, my husband always inhalates just before he gets a cold, it's really like when the pines rustle on the rocky slopes, don't you scent the smell of ozone, of resin? And that blue fiery discharge of neon, it's a cure in itself, your colour is blue, that eases away all the hurly-burly of life, quietens the nerves, retards the flow . . .' I ran on, holding in one hand that beautiful appliance full of inhalating oil and in my right hand still squeezing the rubber bulb which drove the air through the ozone and oil chamber of the inhalator . . . and everything I said Dr Gruntorád repeatedly blissfully after me, smiling blissfully too, and I heard the swing door from the office give a clack, then the key turned in the door and Francin came in, ghastly pale, and he cried out softly, 'What are you up to in here!' And I took fright and squeezed the rubber bulb, and the doctor never finished repeating after me, '. . . pines rustle on the rocky slopes . . .', he sat bolt upright and yelled out, his whole face was drawn and suddenly he was years younger, he jumped up and jigged his legs about in a funny way and felt for the door-handle and rushed out, and Francin followed after him with clasped hands, 'Chairman, forgive me!' But the doctor went on jigging his legs about and ran over to the maltings and into the maltings and down the stairs to the malting floors, there he ploughed through several mounds of barley, the maltsters stood with their shovels astounded, but the chairman left Francin kneeling in the damp malt behind him and ran out still lamenting up the stairs to the lofts, he ran past the dry heaps of malt, but still that pain in his nose drove him on up to the highest floor, there he ran into barley drying on the grids, into that sixty-degree heat, and he ran back down one floor and across the connecting bridge he ran into the brew-house, several times he ran round the vessel and down the stairs he rushed into the fermenting room, Francin still after him, out of the fermenting room Dr Gruntorád rushed on into the cooling room, the place where the young beer was cooled, he opened the window louvres and ran out on to the roof of the ice room, where the house-leeks were in bloom, Francin knelt down into those beautiful yellow flowers, but Doctor Gruntorád lamented again and ran up the steps back into the brew-house and through the gates he ran into the yard and from the yard he ran over to the stables, the work-men greeted him, 'Good day, chairman! Good day, manager!' But the doctor went on jigging his legs up and down on past the orchard, until he ran in again through the open door into our kitchen and back into the living room, where he slumped on to the settee expostulating, 'Where did you buy that piece of junk? Show me!' And he inspected carefully the ozone inhalator with its atom-iser, then he sniffed it and said, 'What did that oil stuff come in, you dratted woman you? Those pines rustling on the rocky slopes and all that?' He put on his pince-nez, I handed him the little flask and when the doctor had read the label he exploded, 'You dratted woman you, you forgot to dilute it one in ten! You've burnt my mucous membrane ... atchoo!' Dr Gruntorád sneezed, and when he saw Francin kneel and stretch out his hands, imploring him, 'Can you forgive me?', the chairman said, 'Get up, my good man, I'd much rather be the manager of this brewery than its chair-man ...' and so saying, he glanced at his watch and gave me his hand, then he kissed the top of my hand and said, 'My respects.' And he left, re-emerging in the yard in the sunshine, trailing behind him a scent of carbolic and disinfectant and eucalyptus, then he hopped on to the box with feudal lightfootedness, as if all that had happened had only given him added strength, and now I could see it! Now I could believe it, it must have happened just as I heard it, that story, the only relic of which was that weeping willow tree, that enveloped the whole house. The doctor sat on the box, the coachman handed him the reins, the doctor lit a cigarette in his amber holder, cocked his soft light-coloured hat over his brow like no other man could, and grew younger somehow with those reins in his hands, he looked as if he'd just arrived in that carriage from

Vienna, he straightened himself and drove out of the brewery with his stallion, whose tail and mane were trimmed, while the doctor's coachman lolled behind on the plush upholstery of the landau with the guilty smile of a man who will never understand why his master rides on the box with such zest and pleasure, while he, the coachman, sits guiltily behind on the plush seat . . . And Francin paced about the room and jammed his fingers into his brain.

I glanced at my watch, it was time for Boďa Červinka to have finished his little round. No doubt he got his vegetables today for a good price, and overjoyed by his bargain he'll have stopped first on the square at Svoboda's, where he'll have had a couple of gills of vermouth and fifty grammes of Hungarian salami, then he'll have stopped at the Grand, where he's sure to have had one small goulash and three Pilsners, then, to start bringing his little round to its conclusion, he'll have stopped at the Mikoláška drugstore, where, lingering in friendly conversation, he'll have drunk three glasses of brandy. It's also possible, however, that Boďa was so overjoyed at saving two crowns on his bargain purchase of vegetables, that he went on to complete his so-called big round, that is to say, stopping at the Hotel Na Knížecí as well, for a black coffee with Original Jamaican rum, and finally dropping in for a quick one at the special bar of Louis Wantoch and Co., where he had a little noggin of kirsch as a final full stop to his celebration of such a cheap purchase of cauliflower and vegetables for his soup.

After Francin had gone off into his office totally unmollified, I hobbled out into the hall, pulled out my bike and rode off into town, I pedalled lightly with my white and painful foot, but then with each push of the pedals the ankle seemed to gain strength. I leant the bicycle against the wall, and when I peeped into the barber's shop, there on the rotating armchair sat Boďa in a snooze, I went in and sat down on a free chair. Boďa must have done the big round today, because he was giving off a smell of cherry stones, he must have ended up at Griotte Inc.'s. 'Boďa,' said I. 'What? Yes madam?' he said getting up with such a start that he snatched his scissors and started snipping them in the air. I said, 'Bod'a, I'd like you to cut my hair.' Bod'a started in shock even more. 'I beg your pardon?' he stammered. And I said, 'Bod'a, I want my hair cut short like Josephine Baker's.' Bod'a weighed my hair in his hands and rolled his eyes, 'What, this surviving link with the old Austria? This hallmark, which says, "Here am I, Anna Czilágová, born Karlovice, in Moravia?" Never!' And Bod'a tossed aside the scissors contemptuously and sat down and folded his arms and looked out the window and glowered. And I said to him, 'Mister Bod'a, Dr Gruntorád has trimmed his stallion's mane and tail and he recommended me this modern cut against dandruff.' Bod'a was implacable, 'Cutting it short would be like spitting on the host after holy communion!' I said to him, 'Bod'a, I'll sign you a solemn written undertaking . . .' 'Only with that,' said Bod'a, bringing his writing things, and I wrote down on a quarter sheet of paper, like before an operation, that I of my own free will and being in full possession of all my faculties requested Mr Bod'a Červinka to cut my long hair short. And Bod'a, having dried this solemn undertaking by waving it in the air, put it carefully away in his wallet, flapped open the white surplice, pulled it under my chin, bent back my head, and took the scissors, he hesitated a moment, it was like that moment when a circus artiste in the big top is about to do a particularly dangerous feat and the drum rolls and rolls . . . and with two big snips Bod'a sheared off my flowing tresses. It took such a load off me, that my head sank forward on to my chest and I felt a draught on my neck. Bod'a laid the hair on the revolving armchair, then he took the trimmer and shaved off tendrils of hair and side locks, then his scissors snipped in the air, Bod'a stepped back and contemplated my hair like a working sculptor, and at once his scissors started working away concentratedly again. Whenever I tried to raise my head and glance stealthily at myself in the mirror, he pushed my chin down between my shoulder blades and carried on working. I saw him starting to perspire, his face gleamed and he smelt of Jamaican rum and kirsch and brandy with a whiff of not terribly pleasant beer about him, he lathered his brush, and every time I tried to look at myself, he pushed my head down, but I saw that a kind of joy was spreading over his face, a kind of delighted smile, indicating that something was going right. Then he soaped the back of my neck and shaved my neck with a razor, then he dampened my hair and trimmed it back with the razor, and suddenly I felt a bitterness in my mouth and my heart began to thump, now, when it was too late, the hair couldn't be fixed back, I saw Francin, sitting in the evening in the office and penning initial letters with his number three lettering pen and round each initial he sets swirling tendrils and my russet hair coursing in the shape of a lyre, I saw Francin having his hands cut from my hair by Bod'a Červinka, having the purple violet glowing neon comb cut away by him, because now Francin will never be able to comb my tresses out there in the darkened room and luxuriate in my hair, which he fell in love with right back in the time of Austria and because of which he married me . . . I closed my eyes and pressed my chin to my chest and sobbed for a moment, Bod'a touched me twice, but I didn't have the strength to lift my eyes up to the mirror, Bod'a took me tenderly by the mouth and lifted my chin, then he stepped back, and was so tactful that he turned away . . . There in the mirror on the revolving chair, up to the neck in a white sheet, sat a fetching young man, but with such an insolent expression on his face, that I raised my own hand against myself. Bod'a unfastened the surplice, I raised myself up, leaned on the marble table top and gazed at myself, astonished, for Bod'a had sculpted out of me my very soul, that Josephine Baker hairdo, that was me, that was my self-portrait, it was bound to stick out a mile at everyone, hit them in the face like a wagon shaft. By now Bod'a had long since dusted the chopped and fragmented hairs off the gown, mercifully allowing me a chance to get my bearings, to get used to myself. I sat down, still unable to take my eyes off myself. Bod'a took the round mirror and held it behind me. In the mirror in front of me I saw in the oval glass the nape of my neck, my boyish neck, which had returned me to my girlish youth, without making me cease to be a woman, still able to tempt herself with that neck of hers trimmed in the shape of a heart. And altogether that new hairdo gave the impression of a helmet, a kind of cap made of hair like Mephistopheles had when the Martin company played Faust in our local theatre, it looked as if it could be removed from my head, just as Doctor Gruntorád a short while back had taken off the plaster bandaging from my ankle, my hairdo fitted close to my scalp like that plaster did to my ankle . . . And I jumped up, but as I was accustomed to my hair pulling my head back, I nearly fell over and broke Bod'a's mirror with my forehead. I paid, promising Bod'a I'd give him a case of lager for good measure, and Bod'a laughed and rubbed his hands, Bod'a too was invigorated by this barber's feat of his. 'Bod'a,' I said to him, 'did you create it all by yourself?' And Bod'a flipped through the series of modern haircuts in his barber's news, from the fringe of Lya de Putti to the bob cut of Josephine Baker . . . I went out, and a gust blew about my head, although there was a dead calm. I jumped on my bike and Bod'a ran out after me, bringing me those chopped-off tresses in a paper bag, he put them in my hand, those tresses weighed a good two kilos, as if I'd gone and bought me two kilos of eel. I said, 'Bod'a, put them on the back for me, on the carrier, will you?' And Bod'a lifted up the spring of the carrier and laid the tresses down, and when he let the spring fall back on the tresses, I clutched my head . . . And then I rode off down the main street, looking at the passers-by, I saw de Giorgi the master chimney sweep, but he didn't recognize me, I rode on to the railway station, looked at the departure times, but nobody paid me any attention, people thought I was someone else altogether, even though the bicycle and my body were just the same as they were before my hair was cut short. I pushed on the cycle pedals and returned up the main street, in front of Mr Svoboda the baker's stood Dr Gruntorád's carriage, only this afternoon had the doctor finally made it to his tubby mug of white coffee and basket of rolls, which would be waiting for him there every morning, for when he got back from his rural deliveries and grumbling gall-bladders, and now the doctor came out, the coachman jumped down from the box where he had been dozing with his hands on the stallion's reins, Dr Gruntorád looked at me, I bowed and smiled, but the doctor only hesitated a moment, then shook his head firmly to himself and mounted the box and drove off, while his coachman lolled behind on the plush seat. I rode through the square past the plague column, everyone looked at me as if they had never seen me in town before . . . on the parade walk in front of the firm of Katz's, draper's and haberdasher's, a bulldog slept, and a group of ladies dressed in black were standing, with skirts down to the ground, the chairlady of the local civic amenity society was seemingly giving a guided tour to some notable composer, he had a big black hat on like a social democrat. Once I too went round with this amenity society with their skirts brushing up the dust of the paving, in the holy church of St Giles we stood by the closed side entrance and gazed at the floor where not a trace remained, only a memory of how hundreds of years ago there was a dried-up encrustation of blood from that massacre when the Swedes and the Saxons slaughtered all the burghers who had sheltered in there, and then we stood by the only really beautiful, historically valuable Fortna Gate, but we didn't stare at the gate itself, we looked attentively under the arches of the stone bridge, where in the year 1913 the animal-tamer Kludský had bathed his circus elephants, still wallowing there to this day in the waters of the Elbe and squirting water over their backs with their trunks like fire-hoses, just like the photograph in the town museum – for Mrs Krásenská, the chairlady of the amenity society, thanks to her revivifying imagination, sees in this town only that which is no longer visible to the naked eye. Now the lady members of the amenity society took their special visitor across into the arcade in front of Havrda's pub, and they gazed in a moved way at the cement pavement where Frederick the Great had once rested. And then, for the most precious thing in our whole little town, Mrs Krásenská led the famous composer off under her arm to the centre of the square, where on a bench two old-age pensioners were sitting resting their chins on their walking sticks, and the chairlady described and accurately delineated the Renaissance water fountain, which stood there up to the year 1840, when it was demolished, but you would be mistaken if you thought it was the two sitting old-age pensioners that the amenity society members were gazing at, by no means! The chairlady pointed and ran her finger around in front of the pensioners' faces, but what she saw was what she was describing, those wonderful ornaments, sand-stone festoons and the two small half-relief angels on that fountain, which used to be and therefore still are one of the adornments of our town. Ah, Mrs Krásenská, who loves everything which is no more, I was filled with affection for her when I discovered her romantic past, thirty years ago she fell in love with a tenor singer at the National Theatre, a Mr Šic, she used to stand after the performance outside the back entrance, and when the tenor singer came out and chucked away a cigarette end, she pierced that butt with a pin and laid it as a precious relic in a little silver casket, and as she was a sempstress, all day she had to sew, in order to make enough for one orchid, and all week she had to sew, in order to buy a seat in the box, where she always threw down that orchid from a day's sewing at Mr Šic's feet, and when she had thrown him that beauti-ful flower for the twentieth time, she waited for the tenor singer and accosted him and told him that she loved him. And Mr Šic told her that he didn't love her, for the one reason that he didn't like her great long nose. And Mrs Krásenská sewed away for a whole year and for the money she earned she went to Brno and had that great long nose cut off and muscle from her own arm sewn on to the nose cartilage in its stead, out of which in time the doctors shaped a marvellously beautiful small Grecian nose. And so it came about, that Mrs Krásenská stood once more at the rear entrance to the National Theatre, and as she was so beautiful, she could strike up a conversation with the distinguished tenor Mr Šic, but the tenor invited her for a nocturnal stroll and confessed to her that for almost a whole year he had been seeking out a beautiful girl with a tremulous long nose, a nose with which he had fallen in love and without which he was unable to live. And Mrs Krásenská confessed to him that she was the girl with the great long nose, but that she'd had it cut off for the sake of the famous tenor and replaced by the nose which he saw before him now. And Mr Šic raised his hands in the air and cried out, 'What have you done with that beautiful nose! How could you!' And ran away from her . . . And Mrs Krásen-ská took a look at me alongside the Renaissance water fountain and raised her hands in the air and cried out, 'What have you done with that beautiful hair! How could you!' And she pointed me out to our town's precious visitor, and now I knew that my hair belonged to its historical monuments. And I pushed down on the pedals and three lady members of the amenity society borrowed bicycles from outside the Hotel Na Knížecí and pelted off after me, stamping so jealously on the pedals that they easily caught me up, and they pointed fingers at me, 'She's cut off her hair!', and several cyclists who recognized me rode off indignantly after me, passed me as well and spat in front of me, and so I rode on through this moving gauntlet of cyclists, all lashing out at me with their angry looks, but that only gave me added strength, I folded my arms and rode on without holding on to the handlebars, and entered the brewery alone. The cyclists stood with their bikes between their legs in front of the office with its sign, Where They Brew Good Beer, There You Find Good Cheer, and now Francin ran out and behind him the three lady members of the amenity society, pointing at me with both hands.

'What have you done with your hair?' said Francin, holding his number three lettering pen in his quivering fingers.

'Here it is,' said I, leaning my bicycle on the wall, lifting the carrier and handing him those two heavy plaits. Francin stuck his pen behind his ear and weighed those dead tresses and laid them out on the bench. Then he unfastened the pump from the bicycle frame.

'I'm pumped up enough,' I said, expertly feeling the front and back tyres.

But Francin unscrewed the rubber tube inside the pump.

'The pump's all right too,' I said, uncomprehending.

All of a sudden Francin leapt at me, he bent me over his knee, tucked up my skirt and whipped me over the backside, and I wondered with a shock, was my underwear clean and had I washed? And was I sufficiently covered? And Francin whipped me and the cyclists nodded in contentment and the three lady members of the amenity society watched me as if they had ordered this rendering of satisfaction.

And Francin stood me back on the ground, I pulled down my

skirt, and Francin was handsome there, his nostrils flared and quivered just like when he quelled the run-away horses.

'Right, lass,' he said, 'we start a new life.'

And he bent down and picked up his number three lettering pen from the ground, then he screwed the rubber hose back in the pump and stuck the pump in the clips on my bicycle frame.

I took the pump and showed it to the cyclists and said:

'I bought this cycle pump at Runkas's on Boleslav Road.'

ONE-WAY STREET AND OTHER WRITINGS

Walter Benjamin

Walter Benjamin – philosopher, essayist, literary and cultural theorist – was one of the most original writers and thinkers of the twentieth century. This new selection brings together Benjamin's major works, including 'One-Way Street', his dreamlike, aphoristic observations of urban life in Weimar Germany; 'Unpacking My Library', a delightful meditation on book-collecting; the confessional 'Hashish in Marseille'; and 'The Work of Art in the Age of Mechanical Reproduction', his seminal essay on how technology changes the way we appreciate art. Also including writings on subjects ranging from Proust to Kafka, violence to surrealism, this is the essential volume on one of the most prescient critical voices of the modern age.

'There has been no more original, no more serious, critic and reader in our time' George Steiner

BONJOUR TRISTESSE AND
A CERTAIN SMILE

Françoise Sagan

Published when she was only eighteen, Françoise Sagan's astonishing first novel *Bonjour Tristesse* became an instant bestseller. It tells the story of Cécile, who leads a carefree life with her widowed father and his young mistresses until, one hot summer on the Riviera, he decides to remarry – with devastating consequences. In *A Certain Smile* Dominique, a young woman bored with her lover, begins an encounter with an older man that unfolds in unexpected and troubling ways.

These stylish, shimmering and amoral tales had explicit sexual scenes removed for English publication in the 1950s. Now this fresh and accurate new translation presents the uncensored text of Sagan's masterpieces in full for the first time.

'Funny, thoroughly immoral and thoroughly French' *The Times*

THE PLAGUE

Albert Camus

'This empty town, white with dust, saturated with sea smells, loud with the howl of the wind'

The townspeople of Oran are in the grip of a deadly plague, which condemns its victims to a swift and horrifying death. Fear, isolation and claustrophobia follow as they are forced into quarantine. Each person responds in their own way to the lethal disease: some resign themselves to fate, some seek blame, and a few, like Dr Rieux, resist the terror.

An immediate triumph when it was published in 1947, The Plague is in part an allegory of France's suffering under the Nazi occupation, and a story of bravery and determination against the precariousness of human existence.

'Enduring fiction has the power to grow into new kinds of timeliness' Boyd Tonkin, *Independent*

INVISIBLE MAN

Ralph Ellison

'I am invisible, understand, simply because people refuse to see me'

Ralph Ellison's blistering and impassioned first novel tells the extraordinary story of a man invisible 'simply because people refuse to see me'. Published in 1952 when American society was in the cusp of immense change, the powerfully depicted adventures of Ellison's invisible man – from his expulsion from a Southern college to a terrifying Harlem race riot – go far beyond the story of one individual. As John Callahan says, 'In an extraordinary imaginative leap, he hit upon a single word for the different yet shared condition of African Americans, Americans, and, for that matter, the human individual in the twentieth century and beyond.'

'One of the most important American novels of the twentieth century' *The Times*

GIOVANNI'S ROOM

James Baldwin

David, a young American in 1950s Paris, is waiting for his fiancée to return from vacation in Spain. But when he meets Giovanni, a handsome Italian barman, the two men are drawn into an intense affair. After three months David's fiancée returns, and, denying his true nature, David rejects Giovanni for a 'safe' future as a married man. His decision eventually brings tragedy.

Full of passion, regret and longing, this story of a fated love triangle has become a landmark in gay writing, but its appeal is broader. James Baldwin caused outrage as a black author writing about white homosexuals, yet for him the issues of race, sexuality and personal freedom were eternally intertwined.

'Audacious . . . remarkable . . . elegant and courageous' Caryl Phillips

THE RAGGED TROUSERED PHILANTHROPISTS

Robert Tressell

At the building firm Rushton & Co. the bosses and shareholders get richer and richer, while the workmen and their families struggle against poverty, hunger and debt – yet think they can do little to change their lives. Political firebrand Frank Owen, however, is different. He refuses to believe that his masters are his betters and encourages his fellow workers to fight for a new, just society – although convincing them is harder than he thinks . . .

The first authentic portrayal of working-class lives at the start of the twentieth century, *The Ragged Trousered Philanthropists* has inspired generations of political activists and remains a moving paean to human dignity.

'The first great English novel about the class war, *The Ragged Trousered Philanthropists* is spiked, witty, humourous, instinctive and full of excitement, harmony and pathos' Alan Sillitoe